MW00324944

PARALLEL

Truth or Die Series Book One

ALEX CLAYBORN

Parallel — Truth or Die Series Book One
Copyright © 2020

The characters and events in this book are fictitious. Any similarity to real persons, living or deceased, is coincidental and not intended by the author.

All rights reserved. No part of this book may be reproduced or transmitted in any form or by any means without written permission from the author.

ISBN Paperback: 978-1-7350695-1-7
Printed in United States of America

Cover Photograph: Malcolm Wright
Cover Cityscape: Nick Fox
Cover Design: Rene Folsom

To Madeline, Malcolm, Peggy, Donna, Dare, Gran (Debbie), Kevin, Rene and LaDonna. You each hold a special place in my heart for your love, time, support, consideration and input into making this book a reality. Thank you!

Bang! Bang! Bang! Lindsay was jolted awake and sat straight up in bed. At first, she thought she was having a nightmare. It was still dark outside. But moments later, her mother's shrill scream made her realize her terror was real. She was wide awake. She didn't know if she should go see what was happening or if she should hide. She didn't move. She was frozen in fear.

She listened intently. She heard a man's voice, along with her mother's cries. She couldn't tell if the low male voice was her daddy's. He wasn't home when she had gone to bed. Wanting to see him, she got out of the bed and made her way to the door to hear better. Quietly opening her door, she was drawn into the hallway by the hushed voices and crying. She followed the voices, making her way slowly down the hall into the living room.

Her mother stood there, quite a fright with huge tears running down her face, along with her brother who was crying and a man in uniform with a Smokey the Bear hat. He looked at Lindsay, then at her mom. Even at eight years old, Lindsay could tell he was uncomfortable.

The only one who seems to notice her was the man. He looked at her mother again, who was a mess, then back at Lindsay. He slowly walked over and knelt in front of her. Calmly, he said, "Your neighbor is going to come to stay with you and your brother for a little while. Your mommy has to come with us, okay?"

Lindsay was intrigued by his hat. "Where's my daddy? I'll stay with him."

He looked at her with a sadness Lindsay would never forget. Then he turned and looked at her mother. Her mother told him to tell her. He took Lindsay by the shoulders and led her to the couch. Just as Lindsay sat down, the neighbor, Ms. Kirkland, came in with another man who had the same uniform and Smokey the Bear hat as the man standing next to her. Ms. Kirkland was crying, too. The man with the uniform knelt again beside Lindsay. "I bet you are a pretty tough young lady, aren't you?"

Lindsay looked at him for a minute, then blurted out, "When my daddy's with me."

Even at her young age, Lindsay knew something was wrong. "I want my daddy! I want my daddy! I want my daddy!" Each time she said it, she got louder until it was a scream.

Everyone looked at Lindsay, then at each other. How would they tell her that her favorite person in the world, her hero, was dead?

Lindsay couldn't seem to stop crying and repeating herself over and over. Finally, Lindsay's mom couldn't take it anymore and screamed at her, "He's never coming home. He's dead!"

Lindsay will never forget the quiet that fell on the room. She will never forget the feeling of her world shattering in a split second. Lindsay wasn't a girly girl, or a tomboy. She was "Daddy's Little Girl." He was her hero, her favorite person in the whole world.

Life as Lindsay knew it ended. Just like that. Like someone pulled a curtain over her little world and she couldn't see anything anymore that was even slightly familiar. Her world had revolved around her father. When he was home, you would find Lindsay where ever he was. They had been inseparable. No matter what Lindsay was doing, every day at 3:00 pm she would stop and go sit on the step in the front of their house and wait. The minute his car come around the corner and in sight, Lindsay became a different person. Her face would light up, her attitude would change, her world was right.

As far back as Lindsay could remember, it was her daddy who tucked her in at night after he read her a story. Some he would make up because he loved to hear Lindsay giggle. As she got older, he would be gone more and more at night. Lindsay couldn't fall asleep for hours if her father wasn't there. No one noticed and thought her crankiness was just because he hadn't tucked her in the night before. Had her mother bothered to check on her on those nights her father wasn't home, she would have realized. But that never happened. Lindsay's mom always seemed to be jealous of the time she spent with her father. Lindsay was too young to realize that anything was wrong between her parents and she may not have noticed anyway, as long as she was with her daddy.

As years passed, Lindsay realized that her father was also the love of her mother's life. She had never gotten over losing him and every relationship her mother had failed miserably. Lindsay's mother had gone through boyfriends almost as fast as she changed her clothes. Lindsay suspected it was because her mother was looking for her dead husband. Lindsay had never been her mother's favorite. That honor was held by her brother with whom she had always fought. Rather, who had always fought with her.

Within weeks of her father's death, her mother started blaming her for everything that went wrong and her brother used her as a punching bag. Lindsay learned to defend herself against her brother. As they grew older, their fights typically ended with her brother in the emergency room and her mother angry and blaming Lindsay. Lindsay didn't understand why her mother and brother hated her. She didn't have anything to do with her father's death.

As Lindsay got older, she knew there was more to her father's death than anyone had told her. At the time of his death, her mother told her that he had died in a car accident coming home from work. Lindsay had suspected there was way more to that story. There were countless times she would walk into a room and everyone would stop talking and just look at her.

4

Lindsay wasn't sure if it was pity, anger or something else.

When Lindsay was fifteen, she and her mother had a blowout fight. Lindsay's mother had her cornered in the walk-in closet where Lindsay was hanging up her mother's clothes. She grabbed a wire hanger and started beating Lindsay with it. Lindsay's brother came in and watched the whole thing, doing nothing to stop the fight. Lindsay finally had enough. As she grabbed the wire hanger from her mother, her brother pounced on her. This was the final straw for Lindsay. All the years of being ignored and beat on came to a boil. She shoved her mother down and proceeded to have a knockdown drag-out with her brother. Her mother had no choice but to call the police when she couldn't get the two of them to stop.

When the police arrived, they took Lindsay away. The ambulance took her brother away, to the hospital. Lindsay would later learn that she had shattered her brother's cheekbone. By this time, Lindsay figured he got what he deserved. All those years of fighting hadn't done much damage to Lindsay except to make her stronger and to learn to defend herself. Her mother told the police that Lindsay was full of anger since the passing of her father. How dare she blame Lindsay or her father? She had always been jealous of Lindsay's relationship with her father and her brother hated that she was her father's favorite. That's why this didn't make any sense. They should have been happy that Lindsay was devastated. They were both so full of hatred and anger towards her.

Fortunately for Lindsay, Harold showed up to get her out of the police station, so she wouldn't have to go home with her mother and brother. He had flown up immediately from Miami when he got the call that Lindsay was in police custody. Harold took Lindsay to live with him and his wife. Harold was one of her mother's ex-boyfriends, and the closest thing to a father Lindsay had, for a short amount of time.

Lindsay wanted to ask Harold about her father, but it seemed every time Lindsay brought him up, Harold scurried off to do something else, apologizing and saying they would talk later.

Lindsay wasn't stupid. Harold feared nothing. Except for the mention of her father. There was definitely more to this story. And Lindsay would find out how much more.

As Kendall walked along the dark, deserted country road, she was nervous. She still couldn't shake the feeling of being watched. She had felt it all day. Now this. Her car had just been serviced last week. She was a fanatic about keeping the maintenance up to date. She never wanted to be stranded. Yet, here she was. Alone, in the dark and unable to shake this feeling. Her cell phone having no signal was as strange as her car breaking down.

Kendall wasn't feeling sorry for herself but she did some musing to keep her mind off of her situation as she walked down the road. Her graduation day should have been exciting, surrounded by friends and family. The only problem was, she didn't have any friends and she didn't have a real family. She was raised by a mother who could not have cared less about her. She kept people at bay. She had always been liked by everyone, although she just didn't let anyone get too close. She had always done her own thing. If you wanted to come along, hurry up. If you didn't, see ya' later.

She had only been walking a few minutes and was about to throw her fear away and get through this faster by breaking into a run when a car came up behind her. She knew everyone in town and knew what they drove. It was hard to see much more than the blinding headlights. What in the world. She had stopped walking and had turned around. The car had stopped a little too far behind her for her to say anything. They weren't getting out and they weren't moving. Kendall wondered which fool from school this was.

She started walking towards the car when the car started backing up. She stopped walking again, put her hands on her hips and yelled, "Come on, stop fooling around!" She expected them to start blasting music any second. She hated these little games.

She started walking towards the car again and again, the driver backed up. Kendall wasn't playing this game, out here in the dark. She hated the dark. She turned around and started walking away. The car started moving again, towards her but very slowly. She turned around to look at the car and it stopped again.

That feeling about being watched was really strong now. She broke out into a run towards the car. It backed up again and this time fast enough that Kendall wouldn't catch it. She figured she could at least get back to her car and shut herself inside of it.

Kendall saw the headlights of the second oncoming car about the same time as the driver of the car in front of her. Kendall stopped. The car stopped. The second one was coming pretty fast and Kendall wondered if she should go left or right to avoid what was going to happen directly in front of her when these two collided.

Just when she thought it was absolutely going to happen, the first car nailed the gas and speed towards her. She jumped to the side of the road as the car speed past her. It was too dark to see anyone inside, but she was sure she heard a female yell, "You got lucky!" She raced back into the road to wave the second car down. It was already slowing. Kendall again couldn't make out who it was with lights blinding her. Just as the car came to a screeching halt and the driver's door swung open, she heard a familiar voice holler, "Kendall! Are you okay?"

"Jack! Thank God it's you!" Kendall ran to Jack and threw her arms around him.

"Come on. No time for that. She may come back."

Kendall released him and looked at him but it was too dark to make out his face. "Do you know who that was? How did you know it was a female? I don't even know who it was and I live here. What's going on?" Kendall asked all of these questions as they were getting in the car.

"Slow your roll. Just take a few deep breaths before you exhaust yourself, and me." Jack always thought she was a little too talkative once you got to know her.

"Seriously. And what are you doing here? How did you know where to find me? I knew I saw you in the audience at graduation. I stopped by the house thinking you would be there. No one was, not even my mother.

Big shocker there. She probably forgot I graduated tonight."

"Kendall, please. Let's get your car and get out of here."

"My car is broken down. I don't get it. I just had it serviced."

"I can probably guess what's wrong with it. When people tamper with them, there are only so many things they do."

"Why do you think it was tampered with? Who would do that? Jack, who was in that car and how did you know where to find me?"

"On second thought, we'll call someone to come get it or I'll get it tomorrow."

"Jackson!"

Jack looked at her and laughed. "Why would you call me that. It's not my real name."

"Really? I just figured it was. What's going on?"

Even if Jack wanted to tell her the truth, he couldn't. "Kendall, she's an ex-employee who I let go. She's pissed. She's been following me and trying to show me that she is smarter than me and always one step ahead. She's not and that's why I knew where to find you. I had a tracer put on your car last week, so I would always know where you are. I got in later today than expected and had to make a stop after the graduation ceremony. When I came out of the place, I saw your car stopped halfway to the lake. I also saw no houses on the satellite. By the way, why were you out here?"

"Fascinating. So how will you stop her? I was going out to the lake. I wasn't up for any grad parties."

"She will mess up. Enough about her. I came because I figured no one else would and we need to talk. Face to face. Now that you've graduated, huge congrats on that, by the way! We know you worked hard to make that happen a year early. Now that you've graduated, we are ready for you."

"Thanks! That means a lot, Jack. Ready for me? We? Who's we?"

"The organization. We. Remember when I first met you? You were fifteen and living with what's his name. Well, I told you then that I worked for an organization similar to the FBI. That wasn't entirely accurate. I work for an elite ops organization. We do things others won't. We go places others can't."

"Okay, so after all of our conversations and me telling you I wanted to go into the FBI, why not tell me the truth? You know how I feel about lies, Jack. You know I was lied to about the things that mean the most to me. What would I be doing?"

"You know I had you take those Karate classes and the shooting glasses to be able to protect yourself. Well, there is another reason. It was training. Training for a job offer. Except it's not really an offer. It's a requirement so to speak. We've put a lot of money and training into you for this."

Jack was shocked when Kendall blurted out, "I want to go to college." He didn't see that coming.

Jack sighed exasperatedly. "Kendall, this is what we have been preparing you for. What do you mean, you want to go to college? We have extensive training for you then your first job is waiting." Jack knew the first time he met Kendall, she was going to be a handful and hard to control.

With what they were offering her, he couldn't have Kendall so headstrong and opinionated. He guessed that came with her upbringing or lack thereof, and having raised herself for the most part. She had been making her own decisions for most of her life. Now to explain to her this life would be better than the FBI. He wasn't sure she was going to be so agreeable. She was still young and Jack had tried to convince the boss to give her a few more years.

"Kendall, can you please just hear me out on this? You will never find anything as challenging yet rewarding. Few are as gifted as you and it's an opportunity not many get. You are gifted and we need you. We have been preparing you." What Jack didn't tell her was that she would be doing office work for a little while until she turned eighteen. He knew Kendall would never go for sitting still. It was all she could do to get through school. There was no way she would last in college unless she flew through it like she did high school.

After hearing the job offer along with the dangers and expectations, she asked, "Why not just ask me if this was something that I might be interested in? You went through a lot of trouble and expense for not having a guarantee that I would consider or agree to this "exclusive ops club" of yours."

Jack just looked at her. How would he explain to her that this is what she was raised to do? This was planned for her as soon as her gift was realized. She would be furious. She would demand answers. Answers that Jack wouldn't give her, ever. "Kendall, you said you wanted to go into the FBI. This is a step beyond that. We don't have rules and regulations to follow. We do things our way. You will be one of the best trained and with your gift, you will be invaluable and can make a good life for yourself."

"Yes, if I want to give up control of my life." The next day, Kendall enrolled in college.

If Jack could have foreseen the future, he would have convinced Kendall to stay in college.

L indsay didn't have to wait too long to find out the secrets, or the lies about her father. Some say they weren't lies, but untruths. Call them what you want but Lindsay called them lies.

One night, Harold thought Lindsay had gone out and as he and wife sat discussing Lindsay, she heard the shocking truths. She overheard him telling his wife that Lindsay's father had wanted to leave her mother but only stayed because of Lindsay. When her father had had enough, he told her mother that he was leaving and taking Lindsay with him. Harold also told his wife that Lindsay's father had a girlfriend at the time of his death and to make it all so much worse, she had died in the car accident with him. Harold told his wife never to discuss it because Lindsay didn't know any of this.

In complete disbelief, Lindsay could only walk in, sit down and look at Harold. Harold didn't even bother to ask her if she had heard what he said. Instead, the color just drained from his face, matching the color of

Lindsay's. It made sense why her mother and brother were so angry. They had both known the truth, and both had kept it from her. Lindsay's mother would later claim to not have told Lindsay the truth to protect her. Protect her from what? Herself? Or from matching their anger and killing her brother instead of just defending herself?

From that moment on, Lindsay promised herself she would never lie to anyone. She hated liars. She had seen first-hand how lies can destroy families and people. She didn't promise herself not to control her anger that welled up like a mountain. She wasn't angry at her father. He was dead. She was angry at the people that had lied to her.

Lindsay should have promised herself that she wouldn't take that anger out on anyone else as her mother and brother had. A week later, she got into a fight with a man that was trying to force himself on her. She nearly killed him. It took four cops to pull her off of him. She put him in intensive care and fled the state. Harold didn't want to send her back to her mother, but there was nowhere else for her to go at the moment.

All of this contributed to Lindsay Phillips learning early in life who she didn't want to be and that she needed to control her anger. She also knew she had more than enough chaos and just wanted a peaceful, quiet, drama-free life. She couldn't stomach any more lies, anger and deceit.

AFTER FINISHING HIGH SCHOOL EARLY, LINDSAY couldn't wait to start college. She had thought about getting a job but was more determined to go to college so that she could support herself one day without depending on anyone. She should have known better than to trust her mother who agreed to let her live there so she could just go to college without worrying about an apartment and all of those expenses.

Shortly before Lindsay finished the first semester, her mother told her that she needed to move out because her brother was moving in and she didn't trust Lindsay not to kill him. She really would never admit that her golden child, her son, was the cause of all of the fights. It didn't matter. Lindsay was done with both of them.

Lindsay moved in with a friend and it wasn't long before she met Mark Wills at an interview for a job. He was the owner of the company, a charmer, older than Lindsay and quite smitten with her.

Within a few weeks of Lindsay taking his job offer, he had asked her out. Things progressed quickly. Lindsay had tired of all of the moving, unsettledness and chaos in her life so when Mark asked her to marry him six months later, she did.

Not long after returning from their honeymoon, Mark replaced her at work. When Lindsay walked into work one morning to a new girl sitting behind her desk, she was furious. She stormed into Mark's office and asked what was going on. He explained that he didn't think it was right for the boss's wife to be working as his secretary and he thought she should stay home and take care of him and the house. Lindsay asked him if he had

17

lost his mind and convinced him to give her a different position. She could be quite persuasive when she needed to be. Lindsay settled into her new office manager job but was bored most of the time since she wasn't really needed.

She started traveling a lot, using any excuse she could to get away on adventures. She had no problem traveling alone and enjoyed the peacefulness it brought her. When she was home with Mark, there was usually chaos of some kind. He got more secretive, but Lindsay didn't care. She had learned a long time ago about compartmentalizing and disassociation.

Lindsay and Mark had a great sex life but that was it. When she was home, it seemed that is all they ever did. Lindsay should have been more careful with her birth control. A missed pill or two and she found herself pregnant. Not long after their son was born, Mark became very controlling. Lindsay could stand just about anything but that. After all, she had been doing her own thing and making her own decisions for a very long time.

The night she told Mark she was leaving him, he picked her up and threw her across the living room almost knocking over the baby in his bassinet. Lindsay got up, checked the baby and flew back across the living room, drop-kicking Mark. As he lay on the floor wiping blood off his mouth, he had the audacity to tell Lindsay that he would kill her before he would let her leave with their son. He got up and came at Lindsay and a hell of a fight between the two of them ensued. Mark had no idea Lindsay could fight like that but he also had no idea that she'd learned to protect herself against her brother growing up. Lindsay had moved him out of the living room, through the kitchen and outside during the fight. She ran back into the house, locking the door behind her. After five minutes, she threw Mark's keys out the door to him, after taking the house key off.

The next morning, Mark came home to an empty house. Lindsay and the baby were gone. He vowed to find her, kill her and bring his son home.

K endall's college career lasted one semester. She was as bored with college as she was in high school. She called Jack. Kendall had never heard Jack so furious as the day she told him she was going to college and she had never heard Jack as excited as he was to hear she was ready to go to work. Jack had never met anyone more hardheaded and determined as Kendall. Except for one other person. His boss. It was a blessing in disguise those two would never meet. Jack shuddered at the mere thought of Kendall and the boss meeting. It would be devastating for everyone involved. He couldn't think of one thing worse.

How was he going to tell his boss Kendall had other ideas for her life or at least the immediate future? His boss lived for the day Kendall would join them. He had personally hand-picked Jack to be her "handler" and had arranged their first meeting when Kendall was still a teenager living with a family friend.

Jack and his boss had argued about telling Kendall then, but his boss thought she was too young to make any decisions. So, he made decisions for her, through Jack of course. It was Jack who suggested she take that Karate class in which she excelled and continued to her black belt. It was Jack who suggested the other two forms of self-defense where she yet again excelled. During one of Jack's checkup calls to Kendall, he suggested she take a firearms class so they could shoot together next time he saw her. She was one of the best he had ever seen.

Jack and the boss both knew Kendall's gift made her pretty special. Not many people had a photographic memory and with Kendall's training and other traits, she was invaluable to them

They put Kendall through some quick training because there was a job waiting and she needed to start immediately. It wouldn't have been so urgent had she not taken that six months to go to college that Jack and the boss knew would never work out. She was too restless.

Kendall's first assignment was going to be a breeze compared to what would come later. They had to ease her in and this job was a favor to the boss. The target was a guy who had swindled a lot of people including a dear friend of the boss. It would be an easy one for Kendall due to her ability to disassociate from people and she wouldn't like this slick guy. She just needed to get friendly, build a "friendship" with him to build his trust and gain access to information that would put him in prison for tax evasion and tax fraud. Of course, this would take a little time. The guy wasn't physically dangerous but if he realized what she was up to, Kendall could very well handle herself. Six months on this assignment should do it.

Lindsay had some figuring out to do. She had moved to a new state, where Mark wouldn't find her. She had done some self-analyzing and realized she needed to be careful about her choices. She wouldn't make the mistake again of having "Daddy Syndrome". That was the basis of her relationship with Mark and why she was taken in so quickly.

She found a lovely apartment, a great daycare for her son and a job at a technical college with the perk of free classes. This is where she met husband number two. Brad Daniels.

Brad was a great all-American guy who everyone loved. He was kind and treated others like they had been his friend all of their life. He was laid back, down to earth and casual and not bad looking at all.

Lindsay and Brad had a great relationship and her son was doing well with him. The first year after the wedding, life was good. Lindsay had left the job at the technical college and found a job traveling. The traveling had to be put on hold when Lindsay missed another pill or two and found herself once again pregnant.

After son number two was born, Lindsay traveled again but not as much. She knew while she was gone, Brad was the best thing for the boys. He dotted on them and being a father seemed to make him happy.

Brad did try to make plans to do things to keep Lindsay from traveling so much. She loved the boys but got restless if she were idle too long. She would stay home as long as she could between trips but it took a toll on her and Brad's marriage. Lindsay was torn between traveling and the boys. She figured as they got older, she could travel more. At least that's what she liked to tell herself.

The years Brad and Lindsay were together, they seemed like the typical every day nice couple living the American dream. No one would believe the lies and the lives below those pretty exteriors. Time would show the devil under the exterior façade. If there was a hell on earth, it was named Brad.

K endall was dreading this meeting with Jack. That assignment certainly didn't go as planned. Did they ever really? She may have taken things a little far but she got the job done. And no one died. The idiot went to federal prison for tax fraud and evasion and the friend was vindicated. She could have finished that assignment in six months, instead of two years. She was the only one responsible for complicating it by getting a little involved with the guy. Ok, a whole lot involved. When had she ever been attracted to a narcissist? She usually despised them. What is done is done. There's that lifesaving disassociation she perfected.

"Jack, there is nothing you can say. I know the mistakes that were made and the things I could have done differently. I was still able to do other jobs. The boss got what he wanted. The end result was accomplished. I'm sorry it took longer than it was supposed to."

"Kendall, contrite and apologetic? That's a first.

Never thought I would hear that out of you. I'm not a betting man, but that I would have bet millions on. You can't just do what you want where this job is concerned. There are safeguards and schedules in place so you don't get exposed or killed. Now granted, this guy wasn't dangerous, but we have jobs for you that are going to require timeliness and deadlines. Your actions are going to affect others. There will be times, many times, that someone could get killed! We know you can do this job but to be honest, we are having doubts after the way you handled this very first one. We have an assignment but it's dangerous. Now that we've seen this, we are putting someone else on it, although they won't get it done as fast as you could. You are costing us time and money."

"Jack, please talk to the boss. Let him know my head is the game and I can do it." If he didn't think I could, he wouldn't have put all the investment in me that he did."

Jack had once told her there were no rules and now, he was saying there was. It seemed Jack like to say whatever was convenient to suit his purpose.

"If you only knew. This isn't a game." Jack realized he shouldn't have said that first part aloud. She would ask too many questions. Kendall didn't miss anything. To deflect quickly, "Kendall, we have to take care of the consequences of your last assignment. That's a horrible way to put that. Sorry."

Kendall just glared at Jack and didn't say anything. She didn't want Jack more upset than he already was.

"We have someone that we are assigning to you. He doesn't know he is being assigned to you nor can he ever.

He's a "nice" guy. Easy going. Laidback. He's easily manipulated and you will thrive with that as a home base so to speak. He will put the normalcy in your life and your image. He won't be paid by us and he will never know about us. He can't ever know about us or what you really do for a living. It would jeopardize you. We have researched him extensively. Do you think you can handle this one? You have to realize what I'm saying to you. Do you get it?"

Jack wasn't sure he was getting through to her. He also wasn't so sure Kendall should be trusted. It was a chance they would have to take, and hope for the best. At least the guy wasn't dangerous and if he exposed her at any time, they would handle it.

Kendall hated not being in control of her own life. She would ask Jack again when she could meet the boss. But she knew the answer. She also didn't want to push it with them being uptight about the last assignment. "Yes, I get it. It's now my life. I'm just not sure why I don't get a say in this. You know I am the best judge of people and with one conversation can figure them out."

"I'm going to forget you just said that after the last assignment." Jack wasn't sure he would ever get Kendall under control and wasn't as sure of her as the boss.

Kendall always had it together so the last stint caught him off guard, which no one had ever done. She got under his skin like a bad itch.

Brad hated sounding like he was whining. He couldn't tell Lindsay how much he hated her traveling. "Lindsay, why must you travel with Barbie's wedding coming up? You know how important this is to my sister."

"We both know the only time anything is of any importance to your sister is when it pertains to her. She won't even notice I'm not around. I'll try to check in with her from the road." Lindsay despised Brad's sister, Barbie.

You and I both know that won't happen. Why do you even try to patronize me?" Brad just sighed. He would never understand why his wife and his sister didn't like each other. Neither of them tried to hide the fact that they couldn't stand each other anymore.

"Because it prevents an argument and because I do have good intentions, although as I said, she won't notice." Lindsay made a mental note to send Barbie a text. She knew Barbie wouldn't respond but it would be enough to prove to Brad she had tried. Barbie Daniels was stuck so far up her own ass and Brad's. Baby brother. It was disgusting the way she was with him. Sometimes Lindsay thought Brad was really Barbie's son, which was completely possible since there were seventeen years between them. Brad looked more like his sister than he did his mother. They both had an odd, but beautiful, color of brown hair. Their mother's hair was black. Brad had a wave to his hair that none of the others did. Brad also had dimples that no one else had. Their father was long gone and the one picture Lindsay had seen of him, he didn't have dimples.

Barbie would put distance between Brad and Lindsay at every opportunity. Brad denied seeing it and accused Lindsey of being jealous of their relationship. If Brad only knew. Lindsay couldn't stand Barbie's constant dotting on Brad like he was a two-year-old. Lindsay also couldn't stand how protective Barbie was of Brad. He was a grown man.

"Lindsay, please say you will be back by the week of the wedding."

"Sure, I'll try." Lindsay hated Brad backing her into a corner on deadlines. Some she could control and some she couldn't. This trip was probably going to be the latter. She was good with missing all of the wedding festivities. She didn't think she could make it through Barbie's special time without vomiting.

"You know we have to get the boys their suits for the wedding. Barbie wants us there to help her pick them out."

"Barbie wants you there to help pick them out. Just

be agreeable because she will get whatever she wants anyway." If Lindsay said she like black, Barbie liked blue. If Lindsay wanted Chinese, Barbie's favorite, Barbie would say she was sick of it and wanted subs, which she knew Lindsay didn't eat.

Lindsay hadn't yet figured out why exactly Barbie hated her. She didn't care because the feeling was mutual. She would figure out Barbie's hatred sooner or later just because people fascinated her and she loved figuring out what made them tick. Maybe Barbie didn't like Lindsay because she thought Lindsay was a threat to her lies. If Lindsay found out Barbie was lying, she would be the first one to call her out on them. Everyone knew how much Lindsay hated lies. Although, Lindsay had a few "untruths" of her own.

8

Kendall couldn't believe they assigned her to this place to "accidentally" meet her cover guy, whom she now called Mr. Cover in her own mind. There was no doubt he would be a geek and she didn't see herself hooked up with a geek. Plus, geeks were too smart for their own good. Hopefully, he didn't have much in the way of common sense.

Meeting him would turn out to be one of the easiest things Kendall did. Another guy started chatting with her and invited her to breakfast. Just Kendall's luck, Mr. Cover was a smoker as was her new friend. While the two were in the smoking lounge, she popped in with a question for her new friend and added, "We can discuss it over breakfast." Looking at Mr. Cover she put on her most alluring smile and asked, "I would appreciate your input as well. Would you like to come with us?" The new friend didn't seem impressed but Kendall was only here to impress Mr. Cover.

Kendall couldn't wait to tell Jack how easy this was.

Jack wouldn't be surprised. How many times had he told her to turn her charm on to get what she wanted? Kendall wasn't comfortable doing that because she very seldom needed anything from anyone. This was a big one though. She needed this guy for her cover and life of "normalcy." Honestly, she didn't know why they had to burden her with a man. If she could remain single, it would be easier for her all around. This one was at least easy on the eyes. Besides, she didn't plan on being around often so he would do.

The whole romance thing happened quickly and effortlessly. Kendall liked the geek and if she had to have this "normalcy" it wasn't so bad with this one. They moved in together pretty quickly. Jack was rather impressed at her speed and Kendall hoped it dulled the memory of her first assignment."

He didn't complain about her traveling, at least not in the beginning. She was grateful for that. If he knew what she was really doing, it would have been a whole different ball game.

9

L indsay made it back right before Barbie's rehearsal dinner. She was exhausted from her trip and the last thing she wanted to do was attend this wedding. There was no way to gracefully bail-out. She had to suffer through it. It was just as well. The questions would be endless otherwise.

Things went smoothly for a little while after that. Then Brad changed and tried to control things, which Lindsay found laughable because Brad could barely decide on what to eat or what shirt to wear. Brad tried to convince her to take a job closer to home so she wouldn't be traveling as much. He knew Lindsay liked to travel and this job was a bonus.

Lindsay couldn't help but wonder why men changed. They started out great but somewhere along the way, they became controlling. Mark and Brad were like night and day, but in the end, both became controlling or tried to.

To salvage what she could because of the

convenience of the marriage, Lindsay took a job closer to home, just to appease Brad for a minute. She put long days into her legal job. At first, it was satisfying although she couldn't stand the drama from the catty girls in the office.

When one of the attorneys who shared office space with her firm needed a side chair in court, she offered to do overtime for her firm if they would let her help the other attorney out, at no charge. She loved that people were so pliable and she was so persuasive. It made her life a little easier and got her out of the office away from the catty girls.

On the first day of court, Lindsay was just coming out of the ladies' room on the second floor of the courthouse. As she walked toward the attorney and his client, who were waiting outside the courtroom, gunfire rang out from the floor above. Several judges had their chambers on that floor and there was a mezzanine from which one could see straight down to the floor that they were on. Someone started screaming, "run" and all chaos ensued. Lindsay was able to make her way around the corner into the stairwell without anyone noticing.

She had considered bringing her gun into the courthouse just because of the shady area they had to walk through to get to the courthouse, but because of security, lax as it was, decided not to. She was up for a new challenge and albeit bored with life at the moment so that may be what caused her to react.

Lindsay made it up the flight of stairs just as the second gunshot rang out. She peered through the window of the door leading from the stairwell to the third floor. She saw the gunman running towards her. Luckily, the area he was coming through was empty. There usually were not many people around as this was Judges' Chambers. As he came through the door, she caught him off guard and was able to grab his gun arm and wrap it behind him. In the struggle, the gun went off. Damn it. She instantly noticed the blood on his back and he hit the floor hard as she let go, sending the gun flying down the stairs. Knowing he was no longer a danger, she fled down the stairs, kicking the gun further around the bend in the stairs. Then she flew down two more flights of stairs.

Lindsay met the police on the bottom floor. With guns aimed at her, they told her to stop. Once they realized she was unarmed, they asked if she had seen anyone in the stairwell. She told them no, she had been frozen with fear one flight up for a few minutes before she realized that the gunman could come down the very stairs she was hiding on. She also told them that she did hear clanking above. Then she thought to herself, thankfully, there were no cameras in the stairwell. But Lindsay knew they would review the hallway cameras and see how long she had been in the stairwell. She just didn't need the publicity.

"Hey Kendall, are you okay?" Jack had a funny way of connecting every time something happened around her, even if it wasn't during the work she did for him.

"Yes, Jack. Why do you ask?" She knew the answer to that and he knew she never asked a question she didn't already know the answer to. Except one.

"I heard about the courthouse shootings earlier today." Kendall thought to herself, "Of course, he did."

"I was in a courtroom when it all went down. I'm safe and sound. Didn't think I was in danger in the courthouse, which I am thinking is why you put me there. Having second thoughts?" Please let him be having second thoughts. She could hope. But she knew better. Jack knew she could handle herself. Hell, she had been since she was practically a toddler.

"No such luck for you, young lady. This is an important assignment even though there are no death-defying actions needed. Well, there shouldn't have been. Are you sure you weren't involved? There is chatter that there is more to this than appears. They think someone met up with the shooter in the stairwell and stopped him short of his shooting spree. Sounds like something you might do." Jack knew that Kendall had a very hard time sitting still and she couldn't resist a little chaos to keep from being bored.

"Sorry, Jack. No heroism from me today. Bored as watching paint dry." Jack hated that he couldn't tell if she were lying. He could everyone else, but not Kendall. "About that meeting with the boss, when is it happening? I think if he could meet me, he would give me more to do. Sometimes these assignments bore me to tears. This is one of them. My "cover" is boring as hell, too."

"Kendall, not every assignment is going to be undercover, in the dark. Well, they are all undercover, but not in the dark. We trained you in self-defense so that you could always take care of yourself. We sure as hell didn't train you in sharpshooting so you could go around shooting people every day although you may find that entertaining. Do I need to remind you why we trained you and what you are doing for us?"

No, she very well knew it was because of her photographic memory. She suspected it was because she was also very independent due to her upbringing, or lack thereof. She didn't depend on anyone and didn't like to be in a position to have to. She also liked to travel, and as of late, was not doing much of it.

"Jack, I know very well why I am here and what I am here for. What I don't know is why I cannot meet the boss. The only unanswered question of my life appears to be what the big deal is in my meeting him. Are you afraid one day I will be caught by the enemy and tortured to tell? Hmmm, you did train me in negotiations which I have not really had the pleasure of using yet. Let me start now, with you, with meeting the boss."

"Kendall, we've been through this a million times. I don't know what your fascination is with this. You know it will never happen. There is no reason for a meeting. There never will be. Please let it go."

Jack knew this just made her want to meet the boss more. She loved intrigue but there was no way around this. He just hoped she would let it go. Maybe it was time to give her more than the law firm job. He knew she was getting restless.

"Look, finish up finding the information on those three clients and we can move on. Before you ask, no you cannot just break into their offices or their homes. It's not there. We already looked. And your "cover" is not for excitement. He's for normalcy."

She hated it when he knew what she was thinking. They both knew the information wasn't going to be sitting in a nice, neat, tidy file somewhere. The law firm's clients' phones had been tapped but they were overly cautious. She had been working on gaining the trust of each of them and their attorney. All of them were guilty as sin. "There's a meeting next week. I'm trying to give myself a good reason to sit it on it but I may need more time to build more trust. Or we could just bug the attorney's office. He would never expect a second try on that."

"That's too easy. Are you sure the meeting is going to be in his office?"

"Good point. It is scheduled to be but let's hope it's not. It would be easier for me to follow him to another destination than to get into that meeting at this point."

Kendall had her own plans about how to finish off this assignment and move on before she died of boredom. Jack would never approve. Jack would no doubt find out but as long as it was after the fact she didn't care. She hated to make him angry but it seemed no matter what she did unless it was following Jack's orders to a tee, it angered him.

There were really two questions Kendall didn't know the answer to. The first being why she could never meet the boss, Jacks' and hers'. Jack knew she wanted that answer and he couldn't give her a solid reason, which just made her more curious. The second question, which she would never ask Jack was why he kept her. She couldn't figure out why he just didn't let her go. Let her go to live her own life and do her thing. Granted, they had put a lot of training into her. There was her photographic memory to consider. The percentage of people who had one was extraordinarily low. There was that plus her independence and street smarts. Kendall would figure this out.

L indsay was happy Brad was so wrapped up in himself and barely talking to her that he didn't ask about the courthouse shooting. Lindsay was very unhappy with this marriage, regardless of the convenience it provided. It was time to move on.

The day Brad came home and was actually interested in her was the day Lindsay was planning on telling him that she was leaving. She told Brad that she would give him time to adjust to the idea, along with their sons. She also told him to come up with something for child support that was reasonable since she made more than he did. She was hoping that she could just walk away with a nice, neat agreement.

That would have been too easy apparently and had Lindsay seen the future she would have killed Brad that night and claimed self-defense. He grabbed her and put her in a chokehold. Lindsay didn't think Brad had it in him. The tighter he put his hands around her neck, the harder she laughed until Brad finally realized she was laughing and let her go. He just looked at her with an expressionless face and declared that the only important thing in his life from that moment on was to make her life a living hell.

Lindsay again wondered about men. What was it that made them change and what was it that made them violent? Her brother used her as a punching bag, then her first husband got violent when she told him she was leaving him, now Brad.

Lindsay didn't think Brad had it in him. The only reason he had his current job was that she had done his resume and sent it out to various employers until the current one contacted him. All he had to do was show up at the interview. If he couldn't handle doing his resume and sending it out, she doubted he would put the effort into making her life a living hell.

In and out of court eleven times in five months is how that divorce started. Brad even managed to get into court before her so he became the Plaintiff. Lindsay did have to wonder how they got here. She loved to travel. He loved to stay home and take care of the boys. The rest was easy or should have been. Brad didn't come alive until the divorce. Had he put that much into the marriage; Lindsay could have withstood it. It didn't help that dear Barbie was at every court hearing. Lindsay did not doubt that Barbie was behind a lot of the never-ending demands that Brad seemed to have.

The first two years of the separation were a whirlwind. Court seemed to drag on but life seemed to have picked up. Lindsay got a great job at a different law office and was doing well. When she didn't have the boys, she was out with her friends or traveling.

About three and a half years into the divorce, things were so bad three of the lawyers she worked with called her into the head of the department's office. They were incredible to work with and had let Lindsay off on days that she needed to be in court, which was quite a few. Lindsay didn't confide in many people but had become good friends with two of these attorneys. They always took an interest in Lindsay and the boys and how court was going. With no nice way to put it, the department head was straight forward, "Lindsay, this is a personal conversation and has nothing to do with work. If we are out of line, please let us know. The three of us think the world of you, professionally and personally, and we know you are going through hell with the divorce and we are concerned. Yes, we have been talking among ourselves about you. Completely out of genuine concern for you and the boys. There is no nice way to ask this and the three of us are thinking it and just not sure you have thought about it. Do you think Brad would harm the boys to get to you? We know everything he does is to get to you and we all know how tough you are, and Brad knows it. But he also knows the only way to get to you is through the boys. We've seen him use them enough to do that."

Lindsay had the same thought many times. She couldn't let herself dwell on it because she would do something lethal to him first. She hated the ways he used the boys to get to her. They were going to grow up really messed up from this custody battle. Lindsay had also thought about all of the ways she could avoid jail but hadn't found one yet. When it came right down to it, Lindsay never wanted her boys to look at her and ask her if she had anything to do with his death. That is the only reason Brad was still breathing.

"Kendall, you can't be serious! Can't you just pretend? What the hell am I thinking asking you of all people that." It was rhetorical. Jack was convinced Kendall's sole purpose in life was to see how much she could frustrate and frazzle him. He believed she was put in his life to tie him up in knots. To see how close to the brink she could push him.

Kendall had taken all she could take of that one. It was surprising she put up with it all as long as she did. Jack of all people knew when she was done, she was done. "Jack, I do not need someone holding my hand. I do not need someone around all of the time. I do not need anyone. I certainly do not need anyone complicating my life or making me miserable. I have you for that. Not the miserable part, but the complicating part." Kendall chuckled to herself. She never let Jack know what she was thinking and it drove him crazy. He could rarely read her anymore and she usually left him guessing. She should have this time, too.

Jack thought about asking her what she meant by that for a nanosecond then thought better of it. He didn't want to know and he didn't want to have a conversation that might lead to a non-professional one if that is what Kendall was referring to. He could never have a personal relationship with her. He knew things he wasn't willing to tell her and she would never forgive him, at least from a personal standpoint. Professional standpoint he could handle.

"Ok Kendall, do what you want because you will anyway. I'll take care of any problems coming out of this. By the way, I'm not your cleaner."

"Then stop putting me in situations that are going to bore me and get messy because you involve stupid people."

There were a few close calls over the next few years as the cases were getting more dangerous all of the time. Even more dangerous than the three clients and their crazy attorney a few years ago. Kendall managed to gain their trust and get herself into that meeting with the four of them. She had mentioned to Jack about wearing a wire. He told her not to chance it and based on data to date, she wouldn't need it. Just her photographic memory. Jack was right. The meeting was non-verbal. Everything was on paper, including the correspondence between them and the bank account numbers money was being filtered through. Those guys and their attorney were now in prison for drug trafficking, extortion and bribery.

Most of the work Kendall did for Jack and the company was quick in and outs. She had taken a few "real people jobs", as Jack liked to call them, as a means to get close to perps but those pretty much bored her. She hated building trust with people because it did come easy to her and at the same time, it bored her. The level of trust that she needed to build though, was sometimes time-consuming because these people were so guarded.

She did also take them as a smoke screen so that no one ever knew what she did. She wanted more challenging things to do. If only Jack would introduce her to the boss. Kendall would never give up on that because curiosity was killing her as to why this was so difficult. Nor did she trust Jack to report to him where she was concerned.

JACK SENSED KENDALL WAS GETTING BORED AND ANTSY again. Why he didn't just give her adrenalin-inducing jobs or people, she hadn't figured out yet.

"Hey, Kendall. This is a happy call. We've got something for you and it's something new. We think you are ready. It's also over the long Thanksgiving weekend. You'll be in Mexico with a hot husband. Tall, dark and handsome."

"Jack, as flippant as you are, it doesn't sound all that exciting. Do tell."

"Actually, you are going as Mr. Cabrera's wealthy wife. Get your ball gowns and stilettos ready." The last thing Jack said to her was, "Be safe."

Six days later, Kendall found herself being escorted around Mexico's finest and wealthiest by her "husband" from their Argentina site. And being hit on by the host of the biggest party. She found it odd that the host would be looking at her like that with her "husband" right beside her.

"Mrs. Cabrera, I wish to show you my most prized artwork. Shall we?" as he put his arm out to escort her away from the crowded ballroom, and her husband.

"You have a remarkable collection. Most impressive. I'm intrigued to see your most prized. Is it not in the ballroom or the lovely sitting room we were in earlier?"

"Oh no. It is my most treasured piece and kept in the most special of rooms." He led her down a long hallway, into the grand room, and up the astounding staircase. As they walked along the second story balcony, he amused her with the story of how he won it in a game of chance.

Nearing the end of the balcony on the second floor, one had to go left or right. As they turned right, there was another balcony. This one overlooked the back part of the house that looked out onto a beautiful lake with several fountains. The rough terrain and the mountains off in the distance behind the lake were impressive. Kendall stopped and admired the view. "Senor, it is breathtaking! You have a gorgeous home." Kendall was taking in the layout of the house, which had been renovated. It didn't match the blueprints she reviewed before this trip. She was also stalling for anyone who might be following them. Or trying to. Security was tight.

In the middle of the balcony, the wall was inset with two huge wooden doors, which they entered. It was the master bedroom. Pulling her into the room further, he shut the doors and locked them. With three long strides, he caught her up in his arms and tried to kiss her. Had he lost his mind! Struggling to pull away, Kendall asked him just that.

Letting her go slightly, "You want me as badly as I want you. You haven't taken your eyes off of me since you arrived three days ago. I shouldn't have kept you waiting." Just as he was saying this, a maid entered into the expansive room and tried to get out without being seen.

Pointing behind him, Kendall said, "Excuse me while I freshen up and you can deal with her." Kendall entered the door that the maid had just come through. There would be no escaping from the bathroom and no other option. She gave him a few minutes to deal with the maid. As she went back out into the room, he had his back to her and turned around just in time to catch Kendall's arm coming up to what he thought was wrapping her arm around his neck to lean in for more attention. Kendall got the end of her pen in his neck and he instantly knew she stuck him with something. He felt his body going numb.

"Am I going to die?" She could see the fear on his face. She knew of his criminal background and behavior. She couldn't imagine what he must be thinking that he would die at the hands of a woman in his bedroom.

"No, you will live, this time, but you will be out for a few minutes and won't remember why you are here or bringing me here with you."

She waited another ten seconds then helped him slide down to the floor. Before leaving the expansive bedroom, she searched through drawers and nightstands and the adjoining office. As she made her way out of the double doors back onto the balcony, she went left to continue to the far end where the there was a second staircase. There were to many cameras in this house to wander off and call attention to herself. She was able to slip back into the ballroom from the opposite side of the house. When she approached the security guard, she explained that the Senor had a stomach issue and would be down shortly. Such a beautiful painting. As much as she wanted to shoot him, she could not. This time. As soon as she was back to her "husband," she insisted they leave. She got more than they bargained for from his adjoining office off the master bedroom. Jack would be pleased with her for finding a "black list" of the Senor's, along with contact information of his associates.

13

Now into the full swing of being single, Lindsay was rather enjoying life. The weekends she had the boys, it was just her and them. The weekends they were with their father, she was out with her girlfriends or working. She enjoyed her job and it allowed her lots of flexibility.

Standing in their favorite bar Courtney asked Lindsay, "Why do you always leave the bar with ten phone numbers, Lindsay?" Courtney and Robin could never figure out why they were leaving with none and she had ten.

"I don't have a neon sign on my forehead that says pick me or marry me. I swear they can spot the two of you a mile away." Lindsay grinned at them to soften the blow. She enjoyed going out with them but sometimes it seemed like they couldn't relax and have a good time if they didn't meet a new guy, which they rarely ever did.

"Maybe so Linds, but you also have the "get away

from me, I'm not here for you" look. That look scares us. Why doesn't it scare men off? It seems they like it."

"Because Robin, they think I'm a challenge." And she was. The last thing she really wanted was a boyfriend hanging around with a list of demands that she wouldn't put up with. Besides, Lindsay had two ex-husbands who vowed to kill her, or at the very least, make her life a living hell and from what she could figure out, just because she left them. She wasn't in a hurry to repeat either of those two mistakes.

"That you are. When is the last time you dated? I mean really dated."

Courtney had been married at one time and had a son about Lindsay's oldest sons' age and the two were friends. Courtney had hoped for husband number two but was having no luck. Courtney had a beautiful custom-built home, along with a barn housing several show horses. She was hoping to find a man to share all of that with.

Robin was straight-up crazy. Tall, blonde hair and an ex-husband with whom she was still in love. She was one of the sweetest and most fun people you could meet unless she was off of her meds. She drove Lindsay absolutely crazy. It never failed that they would start out at their favorite bar, having a few drinks and Robin would want to stop by her ex's bar. This meant a bar fight every single time. The ex-husband's newest girlfriend not only looked like she could be Robin's sister, but both had a temper and a jealous streak a mile long. Robin just wanted someone, anyone to love her. Any man would do.

Lindsay was just about to remind Courtney and Robin of her two exes when she looked up and saw someone. Instead, Lindsay said, "Look at that one. Now that one I would talk to. He's built rather well." Lindsay was rarely attracted to anyone. She rarely paid any attention to men in general, except to be sure they kept their distance from her.

"He's pretty skinny." Courtney gave her a disapproving look that wrinkled her face and made her look crazy.

"Courtney, look again. Look at his arms. He definitely works out. I'll take that one. There's something different about him."

"Lindsay! I have never heard you say that. I didn't think you had it in you. I truly thought you were done with guys. I'm going over to let him know." Off Courtney went on her mission with Lindsay calling after her, "Don't scare him off for crying out loud!"

Courtney must not have said the right thing. She came back by herself. "He has to work up the nerve to talk to you."

"For the love of God, what did you say to the poor guy? You probably scared him off." Lindsay could just imagine what Courtney said to him. It probably went like this, "Listen, you hurt her and we kill you. You mess with her and we kill you. You be nice to her and we'll be nice to you. She hasn't made a comment about a guy in three years and you are the first. Don't screw up."

"No, actually he said he noticed you earlier but you are so gorgeous he was scared to talk to you." Lindsay's looks could be a curse sometimes. Most people thought she was high maintenance just because she took care of herself.

"Yes, that's a great sign of courage. You should have told him never mind right then. Here he comes."

"Hi. I'm Rob Callahan." Lindsay didn't remember much about that first conversation because she was getting a kick out of watching her friends watch them. They probably expected her to scare the guy off with her sarcasm or direct approach to everything. He must have said the right things, she decided he was a keeper. For a minute anyway.

After a few weeks of serious dating and spending lots of time together, Lindsay suspected there was more to him than just his good looks. He had told her that he worked at a large commercial company downtown. He was a plumber and took care of their apartment buildings.

One day while sitting outside on the front porch waiting for Rob, the neighbor happened by. "Hey, Lindsay! It's so cool you are dating my old friend Rob! What a small world, huh? I want to be him when I grow up. He's got the coolest job!"

A plumber. The coolest job. What was she missing? "Hey! Good to see you. Yes, it's a small world. I know right, a plumber of all things." She wanted to ask more but didn't want him to realize she had no idea what he was talking about. As far as she knew, he was a plumber.

"Yeah, last I saw Rob about five years ago, he was an air conditioning guy." As he said "air conditioning" he put his hands in the air and made air quotes. "He is rock solid, not just in that body of his, but a genuinely good guy. I'm so thankful to be back in touch with him."

When Rob got there that night, she told him that they had to go sit in the bar at Three Doors Down because Courtney had another blind date and she had to be there to intervene if needed. He said he was fine with that because he had something to talk to her about and a busy place was better than home in case she freaked out. Never a good way to start any conversation.

After they got to the bar and settled in, Rob just blurted it all out. "I didn't tell you the truth about my job. I can't tell anyone until I'm sure it's safe. I'm not really a plumber. I am a DEA agent. And I need to make a decision about whether I'm staying in or getting out. I was on a case in Miami when it went south quickly. Another agent was shot and killed and we shot and killed a major drug kingpin and his right-hand man. My uncle, who is also DEA, was shot but recovered. There was also an innocent by-stander that was shot. He will be paralyzed for the rest of his life. He's four years old. I don't know why this one shook me but it did. I know it's a lot to ask if you are okay dating me now that you know."

Well, this was a fine mess. "Yes, but if you are working in Miami, I'm not moving there, as much as I would love to."

14

Kendall was able to go over three years without Jack assigning a man to her. Then Jack came to her with a favor, as he called it. One of the guys needed a cover and couldn't do it with just anyone. It had to be someone from the company. Before Kendall could say anything to this new request, he walked in the door. Really tall, blonde hair, blue eyes, gorgeous and built. "You!"

"You!"

"I guess it is safe to say, you know each other but didn't know you worked for the same company."

It was eerie to pass by people on the street and wonder if they were part of your company. It's not like there were Christmas parties everyone attended. There weren't any birthday parties because no one met at an office. Jack had an office but they were only to go there in case of emergency or by invitation. The sign on the door simply said, "Investigator." Nothing like hiding in plain sight. Sort of. They weren't up for general hire.

Tall One, as Kendall nicknamed him, also needed a friend he could talk to. Either Jack didn't realize it or he just didn't put it in the script. Jack knew everything. Didn't this make her his shrink too? She wasn't qualified for this nor is it what she signed up for. Then again, she never really signed up for any of this. She was just led into it at a young age without realizing she was being trained for it.

"So Tall One, what's your plan?" Kendall would have bet before she asked, he didn't have one.

"I would like to tell you that I have a plan but I'm more of a figure it out as I go kind of guy." Great. That makes him dangerous. Dangerous and without a plan. Kendall planned everything with a Plan A and a Plan B and sometimes even a Plan C. She always had an escape route and this clown had nothing.

"Are you working or resting? Let me guess, you don't know that either."

"Nope. I'll take it as it comes."

Kendall had wanted to tell him she though Jack has lost his mind, but decided against it. This would be interesting.

A WEEK LATER KENDALL CALLED TALL ONE. "I GOT A call to go. Did you? Are you on this gig?" Kendall had hoped he was. She rather enjoyed being around him, although everything was chaotic. With the exception of that, it was strange how much they had in common.

"Yeah, I got the call. See you there in thirty. Be safe."

Guess he was working. Kendall hated it when he said that and he always did. The only time anyone else had ever said that was Jack and even then, it was rare.

"Jack, what's up? Are they on the move?"

"Yes, Kendall. We just got word that they have scheduled a shredder for tomorrow morning. We need you in there tonight. It should be a quick in and out. The team is ready. You have already reviewed the floor plans and know what you are looking for."

Kendall didn't like not getting the full story on this stuff before she went in. She was basically told what she was looking for and not much else. This one felt different. The flight was longer than the actual in, review, out. Sometimes she didn't know if they were working for the good guys or the bad guys or both at the same time. She did know she didn't want to get caught and end up in a Mexican jail. Although Mexican coffee was her favorite, she would rather buy it then be served it through bars on a jail cell.

Tall One was on the same flight as she was but they wouldn't be seen together. They couldn't communicate until they reached the meeting destination outside of the city.

Once there, they were given their instructions. It was the office of the same "art dealer" who she had drugged the last time she was in Mexico. At least this time she would be in his offices, not his bedroom. She made the mistake of telling Tall One. He informed Jack he was going inside with her. This is exactly what she did not need. Maybe she would challenge him to a friendly competition once back on US soil.

The team went in as scheduled. She followed up with one agent behind her. They led her to the door of the interior office and she slipped in. It was completely black. She took only a few seconds to adjust. As she neared the desk, she heard breathing. Someone else was in the room. And waiting for her. Why else would they be in a dark office? She continued to move as if she were headed straight to the desk, although her eyes moved in every direction and adjusted to the darkness quickly. She saw him just as she got close enough to match the breathing with a body. She was faster and caught his windpipe, knocking him to the ground and drawing her gun. She snapped on her mini light to blind him just as the door opened and Tall One entered. "Take care of him so I can do my job. And don't say you told me so."

15

Lindsay had what she and the girlfriends referred to as her "court days." It was understood that any day Lindsay had to be in court with Brad, regardless of the outcome, she would be out drinking that night unless she had her sons.

"Hey Rob, I just wanted to let you know I'm out of court and Brad picked the boys up before I could get there after court. He won't let me pick them up. More games. So, since it's Friday anyway, I'm meeting Courtney and Robin at the bar. You are more than welcome to join us. I know you have that meet up with your high school friend." Lindsay regretted calling him the moment he opened his mouth.

"This means you are getting drunk?" Rob couldn't imagine her drunk and wasn't having it without him there.

"You know the only time I indulge is after court. Good or bad. So, yes." Lindsay was not going to play twenty questions and hoped Rob would stop right there. No such luck.

"Since I won't be late with my buddy, why don't you wait for me?"

"Since I'm a big girl and will be with my big-girl friends you can meet us there when you get done. That way you won't be rushed. I know how it is."

"I don't see why you can't just wait for me. Can you at least wait for me to get there before you start drinking?"

"What is wrong with you? No, go do your thing and I will see you when you get there. Because you haven't seen me drunk, I'll assure you that I am a happy drunk unless something happens to piss me off, so be sure it's not you."

Lindsay rarely ever drank. Her friends tried encouraging her to drink a lot more than she did because she became the life of the party and the more she drank, the funnier she became.

Everyone was having a great time at the bar that night. Lindsay was double fisted and the life of the party. She was surrounded by about twenty people listening to her tell a story about one of her antics. Courtney walked around closer to Lindsay and said, "Give me one of your drinks. I'll hold it for you."

"No, I've got it. I'll stop talking with my hands." Lindsay went back to telling her story to her audience.

This time Courtney was a little more forceful, "Give me one of your drinks."

"I've got it!"

"Rob just walked in and is going to be pissed off

with you double fisted. Do you need a drink in each hand?"

"I'm good. He'll get over it." Lindsay turned back to finish her story when the crowd dispersed. "Oh, for the love of God. Seriously."

It was probably the look on Rob's face. "Really, what's the problem?"

"Lindsay, do you have to be double fisted?"

"Do you have to start something over nothing. You knew I was going to be drinking. Please lose the attitude and have a good time. Don't do this. Not tonight."

"What am supposed to think when I walk in and see this and your entourage around you?"

"Are you afraid we are having fun without you or just that you are missing out? Please stop."

"No, I won't."

"Then leave. We are done here." Lindsay headed off to her friends, who had all deserted her during that exchange.

"Ok ladies, back to the fun!" It was obvious by the looks on their faces Rob was behind her and the fun was over.

Lindsay turned around and looked at Rob. Trying not to make matters worse, "Rob, just leave. The damage is done and it's only downhill from here. One of us is going to say something we will regret later."

"But……"

"If you won't leave, I will! Let's go ladies." No one moved. "Fine. I will be outside by myself when you are ready."

Lindsay walked outside and sat on the down on the

edge of the deck next to the front door. Why did they always have to ruin the fun and complicate things? Within two minutes, a guy sat down beside her. She turned to see who it was, knowing it wasn't Rob.

"You may want to move along. It will get ugly in 5, 4, 3, 2, too late."

"I knew it! You couldn't be here with just the girls! How long have you been cheating on me?"

"Whoa, dude, I literally just sat down and don't even know her. She was sitting here by herself and looked sad. I was just going to make sure she was okay." With both hands held up in surrender, the stranger walked off.

"This is why I didn't want you coming without me."

"I have been here before without you and managed just fine. Please leave."

The bouncer, who everyone knew as "Bounce", saw and heard what was happening and moved in. "Rob, just leave her alone. I'll watch her for you. Go back inside." Lindsay had known Bounce for a few years and loved him. He always had her back. She would sometimes go talk to him to scare off the guys who would eye her up while working up the nerve to talk to her.

Just then, Courtney and Robin came out, scooped Lindsay up and left with parting words to Rob, "We are taking her home before it gets nasty. Don't follow."

As Lindsay climbed into bed, her phone was on the third ring of the tenth call. No doubt a tenth voicemail would be left.

That was the beginning of the end. Lindsay did like Rob. He treated her great, the boys loved him and life was good. Except for the jealousy and control that seemed to appear out of nowhere. Nothing had happened to manifest this insecurity. Rob was good looking, built well and treated Lindsay and the boys wonderfully. She kept telling him to get it together or it would end them.

16

"Jack, you are going to have to find someone else to babysit your boy. He needs a therapist too. His head isn't in this." Kendall didn't like how things were going.

Jack knew Kendall didn't have any patience with people that weren't as well put together as her. "You can do this. He's good for you, Kendall. He did save your ass on that last trip to Mexico. And you are really good for him."

"Whatever. He didn't save my ass. He just finished up so I could finish my job. But if something happens, it's not on me. It's on you."

"Great! Now that we have that straightened out, next job. Are you up for a trip to Washington, DC?"

"Sure, as long as I don't have to do anything political. You know I can't stand any of that nonsense." Kendall was the most nonpolitical person she knew. She hated all of the lies, manipulation, and lack of integrity in Washington. She had enough of it with this job.

"It's politically related. But you don't have to attend a party. At least one that you will be seen at."

"Excellent. I know Tall One won't be on this. He stands out like an elephant among squirrels."

"He will. You'll be on your own on the inside and you should be able to slip around easily enough. I'll give you the choice on this one if you want to go in during business hours or after hours. They both have risks."

"Cutting the feeds after hours is usually better, but going in during the day is more of an adrenaline rush. When am I in?"

"The soonest we can go in is next week. Let me know soon so I can get the plan together."

"After hours. Early morning. Should I meet with the boss to get his input?"

"Bye Kendall."

17

"Who the hell is up this early and why are they knocking on my door?" Lindsay was talking to herself and still drunk.

"Really Courtney? The coffee is brewing so I can't drive yet. Plus, I'm no more sober now than when you dropped me off last night."

"Soberer. What are you going to do about Rob?"

"Funny word, don't you think? I'm lucky to be forming words, let alone correct ones. Don't know. He called last night, said he was at the police station and I needed to go bail him out."

"I'm assuming you didn't go if you are still drunk this morning."

"Come on in. I need coffee." As they walked into the kitchen, there was coffee everywhere. "I guess I have not perfected drunk coffee." The pot was still in the sink. And the coffee was everywhere.

"Sit. I've got this. Seriously, Rob was out of control

last night but Lindsay you were pretty drunk by the time he got there and we hadn't been there long."

"I don't think my getting drunk was the issue. He's been acting a little crazy lately. He's got other issues and I'm not sure they involve me. He's projecting. I think I told you about last week when I got home at ten. He was sitting on the couch when I came in the door with the boys. He was furious I was four hours late and accused me of all kinds of horrendous acts. Anyone within a day's drive of here knew there was an overturned tractor-trailer that had the highway shut down."

"What are you going to do? He truly is a great guy."

"So was my ex-husband. But not to me. By the way, in court yesterday, he tried to say that I was harassing him because he's got a new girlfriend who is better than me. As many issues as we've got and the issue of his "Woman of the Week" hasn't even come up yet! My lawyer doesn't want to touch the issue because he thinks it would restrict future boyfriends for me who might want to move in. It's ridiculous. I haven't lived with anyone since we separated. You know Barbie was there to add support." Lindsay was so over Brad and his women. God knows how many he may have had while they were married. Maybe that's why he didn't mind the traveling that she did. She didn't think for one minute he had others during their marriage because he was such a homebody. If he had, she wouldn't have cared anyway. Not like there was much going on between husband and wife the last few years anyway.

"When did he start with the "Woman of the Week?"

"It was within weeks of me leaving. I just brushed it

off as his drunkenness. He was out all of the time. I had a PI following him because he just got stupid. At first, we thought he may have had a girlfriend the whole time but then the next week it was someone new. Then a few weeks later, it was another new one. It hasn't stopped. I told him as long as he was a father first and left the boys out of his new lifestyle, all would be well."

"And he hasn't done that?"

"That's not a question, right? You know how many times we've been in and out of court and like I said, that hasn't even come up yet. As for Rob, we're done. I can't deal with two psychopaths. Actually, it's three psychopaths if you count Brad's sister, Barbie. And if Mark ever finds me, it will be four. Add my mother and my brother in and we have… never mind. I may need to analyze my life a little closer but that would more than likely lead to therapy. Or possibly a padded room."

"It's as I said."

Lindsay looked at her with a confused look and it took her a moment to remember Courtney had a pet peeve with English. "I'm dealing with a life of psychopaths and you are worried about my English? I want to be you when I grow up."

18

Speaking into her body microphone, Kendall whispered, "Tall One, check the stairwell." Nothing. "Tall One. Answer. Tall One. Answer." Kendall knew he shouldn't have been in on this. It was 4 am and she had to wait for him to get there. He held up the team that morning. He was an accident waiting to happen. And now he wasn't answering her.

"Eight nine, this is Q Sand. Go ahead."

"Check the stairwell." As Kendall came around the corner, she caught a glimpse of what she thought was movement. It was so fast she wasn't sure. She wouldn't think about Tall One and be distracted. At least not right now. She pointed her gun and crept closer to the stairwell. Timing was everything.

"Eight nine. Reroute."

This wasn't good. She started for the alternate route out. Once she cleared the exterior door six flights down and at the new pick up spot a mile away, she could be mad. The mile jog would help. She loved this little coffee shop where the alternative meet up was. She actually liked this part of DC with its cherry blossom trees, brick sidewalks, quaint stores, and a welcoming feel. Maybe she would come back for a visit when the cherry blossom trees were in full bloom. She tried to get to DC every year for the cherry blossoms. They were beautiful and made it seem like a new city. Kendall actually loved the city with its rich history and all there was to see. It was the politics that ruined it for her.

Jack was slipping and it was causing her problems. His discretion on choosing these guys was creating drama and problems for her. How did Jack not see what was wrong with the geek and now Tall One. She would talk to Jack about this but she really needed to talk to the boss about Jack slipping on his character evaluations. She was determined she would have more input and choice should she be partnered with anyone again or anyone needing her.

While she was fuming about the geek, Tall One and Jack, she decided she would find out the big secret about the boss. She had been with the company long enough that she should have met him by now.

For as smart as Kendall is, she would never figure out men. It would be one thing if she were choosing them, but she wasn't. If a man can't choose a good man for a job, how would a female? That was something to ponder. Her first boyfriend in high school cheated on her with her best friend. Kendall didn't like him enough to care so there were no lasting effects. She, fortunately, was smart enough to know that not everyone was going to do that just because one did. Besides, Kendall just didn't get close enough to anyone to care what they did.

Jack. He was his own story. He was the one person who Kendall had thought at one time she may have a future with. Not a work future either. He was also the one person who could infuriate Kendall. Sometimes Jack would treat her like she was just a pain in his ass and other times he would treat her like she was special. Not as in work special. Sometimes he genuinely seemed to care about her and her well-being. Maybe he did care. Or maybe he cared about himself more. It appeared he did not want to anger the boss where she was concerned. Why? She would find out.

19

"Lindsay, we have a new trial date. When can you come in to review?" He was expecting her to terminate him. His secretary had offered to call Lindsay and schedule an appointment, but he, as her failing attorney, knew that would only make her mad. Better talk to her now so when she does come in, they could get right down to trial prep.

"I'm glad we finally got one because I was going to call you this week and fire you. You know Brad has been taking the boys every single weekend. I have screamed about this for the past nine months and you have done nothing. I could represent myself better than you have been." Lindsay was beyond fed up with men.

"I know and I apologize. I'm not even going to try patronizing you because we both know you are right. Are you sure you still want to go for sole custody? There's a slim chance you will get it."

"I should fire you just because you don't believe in your own abilities or the merits of this case. Yes, I'm sure. If you aren't, recuse yourself and I'll handle it. By the way, that $10,000 from the attorney fees in interest that Brad was supposed to pay is still showing on my bill. Fix it because I promise you the only way you are going to get it is to get it from Brad. You should never have cashed his check that was made out to me and had "paid in full" on it."

"Linds, you are right. I will take care of it."

"Don't call me that. Only my friends do and today you are not my friend. You want to know when I want to come in and refresh your memory on the issues? How about Thursday at 2?"

"See you then. And I still say you should have killed him off. You would be getting out of prison soon with your Master's degree."

"I'll kill you if this doesn't go as planned. Study up, friend." With that Lindsay hung up on him.

She couldn't believe that this case was still ongoing. She and Brad were divorced, thanks to her. But every single other issue had been reserved. Not one issue with child custody or support was finalized. She had been in limbo with this for years. She had finally let the house get sold for lack of wanting to fight about it on top of everything else. Besides, she moved every two years or so. Not because she liked moving but because of circumstances. She was moving again because they had redistricted her sons' school. Lindsay wouldn't have her oldest going to school in that town. No doubt if Brad hadn't moved a few times, this would be another contention point in court. Brad had moved from an apartment to a townhouse. Her attorney had actually told her she needed to do the same to compete with him. Since when are living arrangements or any other issue in these cases a competition. Besides, Brad's latest girlfriend had moved in with him. She should just handle the case herself. In the last few years working in law offices, she had learned a few things.

Her friends had always said she should be a lawyer. She may have been if she stayed in school. But life happened.

Lindsay was currently at a law firm but not too happy with one of the attorneys. He had a Napoleon complex. They hired her because she had the experience they needed. Indeed, they did. They had a few million dollars of a client's funds in escrow and didn't know what to do with it. She had one word for them the first day on the job. Disbarment. The attorney hated that Lindsay knew more about this stuff than he did.

Lindsay had filled in as a bartender for a friend of hers that owned a bar. He had since been begging her to come work for him. She had been considering it, just for a change of pace. But with court coming up, she didn't think that would be very "competitive" against Brad who was still at the company she had gotten him the interview with. She could imagine what her attorney would say. Bartending wasn't remotely on the pay scale of Brad's job. Since Brad had been at his job a few years now, he was finally making decent money. Not that Lindsay cared. She just wanted a little peace from all of Brad, Barbie and court. Lindsay and Barbie had a few run-ins and because of the boys, Lindsay didn't give her much attention. Of course, this infuriated Barbie.

Either way, it seemed everything her attorney had done was silliness and not going to matter when it came right down to it. She also knew how attorneys could be. They always had to have the best client who had the best house, best job, best everything. It was all appearance and who knew who. Lindsay refused to fall into the legal shenanigans. They were as bad as political ones in her book. She would win this case, with or without her attorney. Not that anyone really "won" when it came to custody battles but getting sole custody of the boys would, hopefully, give her a little more peace where dealing with Brad and Barbie were concerned.

When friends would ask her about which attorney to hire when they found themselves in court, if it were a divorce case, she would suggest opposing counsel's best friend. The friends would want to go find their spouses' attorney's biggest enemy. That was the worst mistake they could make. Then the attorneys ended up fighting each other and clients of each suffered the most. Lindsay would suggest they find opposing counsel's best friend so they could settle the case on the golf course.

"Kendall, I'm sorry for what you have been going through personally. I wish there were something I could do besides the illegal things I can think of." The look on Jack's face should have softened Kendall's comeback.

"That's entertaining coming from you of all people, Jack. Thank you though. There is something you can do for me. Well, two things actually. The first is to stop assigning me babysitters or having me babysit. The second is to introduce me to the boss." With Jack feeling bad and the last couple of other people's screwups, maybe now Kendall would have a chance. Jack was impressed that even considering how things were going, Kendall was able to salvage the assignments, getting the jobs done. But Kendall did thrive on chaos a little bit, even if she wouldn't admit it.

"Done. At least the first part of that. The second part is a weird obsession you have developed. You knew you would never meet the boss. Drop it, Kendall. It will never happen. There is no reason." Kendall noticed he never referred to the boss as he or she, just the boss.

"What's next?" Kendall wasn't happy with Jack's answer.

"You have been pushing really hard in the last few years. Want to take a break and take care of you for a little while?" Was he giving her some free time to do her own sleuthing without even realizing it?

"Does this mean you don't have anything for me or are you serious? You've never offered this before."

"Seriously, go do some things you enjoy and take a break. We can handle things going on around here."

If Jack had known her intentions, he never would have given her a free second.

Kendall knew the only way she was ever going to meet the boss was to discover his/her identity herself. And that she would do. She had been curious long enough. There was obviously some big secret or some serious reason the boss was never met or really mentioned. If it hadn't been so secretive, Kendall probably wouldn't have given it a moment's thought.

21

Lindsay was fed up with the injustice in the legal field and decided a change was overdue. She asked for two weeks off from the firm for a week of trial prep and four days of the actual trial. The bosses balked and she threatened to resign. She won. She got her two weeks' vacation.

The first thing she did was head to her friend's bar and work out a schedule she liked. She was to start the Monday after the trial finished. No one, of course, would know this and when asked in court where she was employed, she could still say the firm. As far as they knew, she was on a two-week vacation.

She needed some fun in her life and was looking forward to having a job that required no overtime, not taking work home and leaving work at work. It was time she started enjoying some free time. She was a workaholic and when not working, she had been with the boys. She had since given up going to the bars with her friends, although those two were still hitting the bars and looking for Mr. Right. They had definitely mastered finding Mr. Wrong. Lindsay had hoped they would find what they were looking for. She kept in touch with Courtney, but only seeing her every few months.

The trial was brutal as trials go. This one was way past due and she was tired of the fighting. Hopefully, this would put an end to it once and for all. Lindsay hated drama and that is what this whole thing with Brad had always been.

No one ever wins in court. Lindsay did get sole custody but the judge gave Brad daily visitation. This would be a nightmare. He gave Brad a free pass to continue making Lindsay's life a living hell, with his intrusive sister's help. She would be making all the decisions such as schools they attended, dentists, doctors, churches, etc. This would put Barbie over the edge. Daily visitation gave Brad an opportunity. What was the judge thinking? At least there would be no more mandated therapy and counseling. That was brutal for everyone. It did explain some things about Brad though. Like he was incapable of making a decision. And his personality was so shallow that he didn't have one. He would pick up the personality of whomever he was interacting with at the time. Most people like themselves so this made perfect sense why most people really liked Brad.

Brad had changed since she left. He was like night and day. If there was anything he could do to infuriate Lindsay, he did it. Even if it hurt the boys. He knew the only way to get Lindsay mad was to mess with them. And he did. Barbie wouldn't hurt the boys but she would hurt Lindsay any other way she could. Lindsay was still convinced she was Brad's mother but didn't care enough to find out. Although, maybe she should. With that information, Lindsay could shut Barbie and her crazy down pretty quickly. Get her to back off.

When the dead roses arrived on Lindsay's doorstep the last day of the trial, for a brief moment, Lindsay thought they were from Brad, but it didn't take her long to remember it was the anniversary of her father's death. They didn't arrive every year, but random years. Lindsay had been convinced her brother had been sending them. Of course, he and her mother denied it, but who else would have her address since she moved so often, usually every two years or so.

22

Kendall didn't have any hobbies as she never had time for much. She did like to read, but sometimes that could be overwhelming with her memory taking pictures of everything. She also liked puzzles, but not the normal kind, the complex puzzles like Jack. She would figure him out and hope this led to information about the boss. Of course, she loved to travel.

The first week, Kendall took care of some unfinished business and stuck around the house, deep cleaning, organizing and of course, planning. She liked to clean and think.

Her first move would be to find out where Jack lived. She knew where the "office" was and had been there a few times. She was currently living in the same city as the office, although on the opposite side. The office was in the business district but not the fancy part. Jack's office was on the outer edge in a one-story building with rows of offices. She lived on the other side in a suburban area of middle-class homes with lush landscapes but few trees.

She would follow him home from the office. Jack's home. She had no idea where that was these days. Kendall had never been to Jack's home. He wasn't married but as for girlfriends, they had never discussed any. She would have to change that.

Naturally, it would be easier for Kendall to have someone that he didn't know follow him but she didn't trust anyone else with this. And you never really knew who was working for the organization.

The first three days of watching the office, there was no sign of Jack. Kendall hated wasting time and reconsidered paying someone. One more day.

One more day paid off. The fourth day Jack showed up. Kendall could only hope that when he left the office, he was going home. She didn't want to be following him all over the city. That would also be quite risky in the event that he made her. That would be tough to explain with her living on the other side of the city.

Around four that afternoon, Jack left the office and got into his Mercedes. Kendall followed him out of the city and to a private airport. This wasn't the private airport the company used. Jack went right through and jumped into a helicopter. He must be on an assignment. There was only one way to confirm since she couldn't very well jump in a neighboring airplane and follow him. They didn't usually take helicopters. They had the company G5.

Kendall found a nice coffee shop and hung out until after dark when the private airport would be less likely to have anyone going through. While waiting for darkness, she pulled out the disposable phone that she had bought earlier that week. She searched the FAA's aircraft registration database. The helicopter was owned by a leasing company, PJ Enterprises, Inc. Research of PJ Enterprises, Inc. led to a larger corporation, Langston Corporation.

Just as Kendall was about to dig into Langston Corporation, a dashing gentleman asked if he may take the extra seat at her table. She wanted to say no, but looking around, it was the last seat left in the coffee shop. It was busy for this time of afternoon. She nodded but was hoping he didn't want to do the small talk thing. But naturally he did. Kendall wasn't good with chit chat, so she sipped her coffee and let him do most of the talking, just smiling and nodding. Kendall had a tendency to be a little paranoid so when he asked personal questions, like where she was from, why such a beautiful lady was alone and if she had family, she easily lied.

Once she was able to get away from the dashing but very talkative, gentleman, she drove back to the private airport, parking as far on the edge of the parking lot as she could. She tucked her hair up under a wig, put on some red lipstick, which she never wore, and went inside.

She approached the desk and pretending to be scared and out of breath, told the attendant behind the desk that someone was outside sneaking around and he may want to call security. He told her Security was on the airfield and to stay put and he would check it out for himself. He was no sooner around the corner when Kendall hurried behind the desk and pulled the flight plans for that day, finding the number of Jack's helicopter quickly. With the flight plans in front of her, she scanned the rest of the logs for the tail number of that helicopter to see how often it flew and who logged in.

She wasn't quick enough to get out from behind the desk when the security guard came in from the airfield and asked her what she was doing and who she was. Kendall explained she had seen someone outside sneaking around and the other guy had gone out to check and she was ducking back there for safety. He ran out of the front doors. Kendall ran out the back doors onto the airfield. She quickly but silently ran along the side of the building towards the front of the airport where she could see the security guard and the other guy talking. Once they started for the door, she started for her car on the edge of the parking lot. Seeing no other cars coming in the entrance of the parking lot, she drove the wrong way out for faster clearance.

Kendall wondered to herself, Philadelphia? What was in Pennsylvania? They hadn't done any jobs there, at least Kendall hadn't. Jack could also drive to Philadelphia in about an hour, in light traffic. Why the helicopter? Maybe PJ Enterprises or Langston Corp. had a job for them? Maybe he was going to meet the boss. She would find out because it appeared Jack was the only one logged in and out for the past few weeks on that helicopter. The only destination was Philadelphia. One thing about flying in any type of aircraft, public or private, is that there are FAA rules and regulations, and recorded logs.

23

Lindsay was excited to get started at the bar. Although she was mostly an introvert and didn't have many friends, due to trust issues and her independence, she was looking forward to putting her sarcasm and wit to good use. What better place to use it than with a bunch of strangers drinking in a bar?

The bar was a bar-restaurant and many of the day customers were regulars from the local businesses and contractors. She got comfortable quickly and was pleasantly surprised to turn over the lunch crowd several times. Then the happy hour crowd would come in and she would spend an hour with them before her shift was done.

They loved to tease her and try to find out more about her. Naturally, she didn't tell them anything. It kept them guessing and intrigued. She was going to like it here just fine.

Lindsay got hit on a lot, which made her extremely uncomfortable and was something she would never get used to. It was a little tough to tell them straight up "no". Her tips depended on her pleasantries. She had made herself a rule the day she started and that was she would not date a customer. That soon became her excuse. Guys said they wouldn't come in anymore if she would date them, to keep her job and personal life separate. That's a great way to lose customers and money.

Lindsay had been there for several weeks and one slow afternoon, she was standing behind the bar with her back to the front door, joking around with a regular customer. As she turned slightly to check the rest of the bar, her heart stopped, she lost her breath and her smile froze on her face. By some form of automatic response, she started walking toward the most gorgeous creature on which she had ever laid eyes. She knew at that moment, her life as she knew it was over.

"Hi. Can I help you?" Breathe. Lindsay breathe, she told herself.

"If it wouldn't be too much trouble, could I get a beer, please." He had the most charming smile Lindsay had ever seen. Those eyes bore right through to her soul. They were green but had blue hues, sometimes making them appear blue depending on how the light hit them or the spark that lit them up. He had the most beautiful color of brown hair and just the right style and length for Lindsay's taste. Lindsay wasn't sure how she didn't reach out and touch it. His skin was flawless, his bone structure was perfect. Oh, and those lips were the perfect color to match his skin tone and the perfect size for the rest of his features. Behind them, his teeth were perfect. Lindsay took all that in just during his one sentence. His face was one Lindsay would never get tired of looking at, or forget.

"The only trouble would be figuring out which beer you prefer." Breathe. Lindsay breathe.

"You mean as a bartender you don't automatically read people to know that?" The teasing grin was more disarming than the charming smile. She was in trouble. If he realized she just read his fabulous face the way she did, he would have probably run for his life.

"I'm a bartender, not a clairvoyant." Breathe. Lindsay breathe, she reminded herself again.

"You win. Budweiser, please. But again, only if it's not too much trouble?" That grin never left his beautiful face.

Lindsay had no idea how she managed to get the beer and put it on the bar in front of him without spilling it. Her hands were shaking. Her insides, brain included, were mush. Good thing the smile was automatic. This one may be frozen on her face forever. The only trouble going on here was Lindsay couldn't think of one thing to say to this earth-shattering, gorgeous creature who was the first person in her life to make her feel this way. She just hoped he didn't see it. She had to know more about this man who was stealing her breath away, but how could she do that without making a total fool of herself, she wondered.

She hadn't seen him come in so she had no idea what he drove. Lindsay did see there was no ring on his finger. He didn't appear to know anyone else in the bar. He was sitting at the bar where no one else was. It was probably a blessing so that when she moved down the bar to wait on others, she could catch her breath. Every time she glanced his way, he was watching her.

On one glance he raised his beer to her and she just smiled back. A few minutes later, he raised his beer to her again. Lindsay knew for most people that gesture meant they were ready for another beer. It didn't occur to her that was why he was doing it. On the third raise of his bottle, the customer in front of Lindsay said, "I think the poor guy is dry and wants another." Lindsay had never in her life been embarrassed, until now.

"Would you like another?" Lindsay had no idea how she had walked down the bar to him or formed the words.

"If it's not too much trouble." There was that grin again. She wanted to tell him to stop it.

"It's no trouble. Let me guess, Budweiser?"

"Unless you have another suggestion."

Lindsay couldn't publicly tell him what her suggestion to him would be. It wasn't beer. Part of her was happy he was having another while another part of her wanted him to vanish as quickly as he had appeared so she could get her senses and her life back. She couldn't have recalled one person that was in the bar nor could she have explained how she continued to work. This time she would be back to him before he would have to ask for another beer.

"Ready for another?"

"As much I as would love to, I better go. Could I get my tab, please?"

Lindsay wanted to tell him no, he had to have

another. Or to make him promise to come back soon. "I don't know. That might be too much trouble."

As she told him the total, he pulled out cash. "We don't take cash. Only credit or debit. See, too much trouble." She was hoping for his credit card to get his name.

He laid the cash on the bar, winked at her and continued sipping his beer. She didn't take his money right then in hopes that he would ask her for change so she would know he was leaving and could see what he drove.

Lindsay had turned away from him to wait on another customer. When she looked back to check on him, he was gone. Vanished. She ran to the window and watched for a minute. The only way in and out of the bar driveway was in the front of the building. He was nowhere in sight nor did any vehicles leave. He vanished as quickly as he had appeared.

"Lindsay, come here." Bret, the cook in the kitchen, called her.

As Lindsay approached the kitchen, "Who.was.that?"

"I have no idea. He appeared at the bar without me seeing him come in and he disappeared the same way."

"I think he is my next husband."

"Bret, stop it. You leave this one alone. You can have my ex-husband."

"No, there is no way he looks like that one. You need to find out who he is or pray he comes back."

Lindsay was walking on clouds for the rest of the day. She couldn't think of anything else.

24

K endall staked out the airport early every morning and every night. Jack usually arrived right at 8 a.m. but left different times of the day. Kendall couldn't sit there every afternoon. Instead of trying to get back inside of the airport, she would see if she could get into the FAA flight logs on-line. It was a last resort.

She remembered the three-letter identifier of the airport in Philadelphia. It was time for a road trip.

Arriving in Philadelphia at the private airport, Kendall was in time to catch Jack arriving and see the license plate number of his car. Kendall loved that with her photographic memory, she never had to jot down anything. Another Mercedes. One at each airport. She decided not to follow Jack but instead see where the license plate registration would lead her.

Tracing the license plate number revealed the owner to be PJ Enterprises, Inc., the same company that owns the helicopter and the address turned out to be an office building. This wasn't what she was hoping for.

Kendall drove to the office building located on 2nd Avenue. It was a fairly plain, no-frills building. She entered the lobby and quickly located the directory. The office of PJ Enterprises, Inc was on the 8th floor along with a few others. Stepping off of the elevator and into a small foyer, there was a short hallway with doors on both sides. She located the office quickly. Most of the offices appeared small.

The office was the last one on the left. A single wooden door imprinted with PJ Enterprises, Inc. No windows. No indication of what they did. Nothing. The other offices all had a window so you could peer in. Kendall tried the lock. Nothing. She didn't dare to try her credit card. She turned and started back toward the elevator.

Just then, a man came out of an office next door. "Can I help you?"

"Oh, maybe. I'm looking for an investigator's office. I thought he told me the 8th floor, and I forgot the name. None of the other office names sounded familiar and I thought maybe this was it."

"I'm sorry, I can't help you. I'm not sure what these guys do, but I've never seen anyone come or go. Maybe try calling them."

"Thanks. Good idea. Don't I feel silly."

"Good luck."

Kendall didn't like dead ends. She would have to figure out what time Jack usually flew back into Philadelphia but for now, she had to get back.

25

The next day at work, Lindsay was hopeful Mr. Gorgeous would be back. It made for a long day waiting until the afternoon to see if he would appear again. Fortunately, she lost track of time with a busy lunch crowd and the post-lunch crowd.

He did it again. He just appeared among the regulars. She didn't see him entering the bar or see him sit down. He was just there. How did he do that?

"Hi again! Budweiser?" The shaking started again immediately upon seeing that beautiful grin and again, Lindsay had to remind herself to breathe.

"Hi. You remembered? Yes, please." He said this in almost a whisper, as to not draw attention to himself.

Lindsay leaned forward and almost in a whisper said, "Don't tell the regulars. They may get jealous."

"It will be our secret." His wink, along with that grin, almost did Lindsay in. Lindsay had never seen a real person this gorgeous. But still, what was up with the physical effect he had on her. They were strangers and had barely spoken a dozen words. This would have to stop.

As Lindsay gave one of the regulars his soda refill he said, "Lindsay, who is the hunk? I've never seen you beam so bright! New boyfriend?"

"Stop it. He's a customer. Second time in. Don't get any ideas."

"I can make you and him happen. C'mon, let me have some fun."

Lindsay hissed between her teeth, "I will cut you three ways, left, right and down the middle. Don't you dare say or do anything."

He backed up in his seat and raised his arms and clamped his mouth and sucked his lips inward, as if in surrender. Naturally, Mr. Gorgeous witnessed the surrender. Luckily, he was too far away to hear the conversation.

Another glance from Lindsay and another raise of the bottle with that charming smile. Lindsay wished he would stop that. "Here you go. Want anything to eat today? We've got some good specials." Anything to keep him around.

"No, thank you. I'll try not to be too demanding. I don't know what you said to the guy down there but you put him in his place. He didn't want more food, did he?" That grin.

"No. Ignore him. He's a trouble maker. I call him "Drama Llama" for a reason."

Lindsay wasn't so sure he didn't hear the conversation and blushed at the thought that he may have overheard. The wink from Mr. Gorgeous only intensified the blush.

On the one hand, Lindsay was glad she was busy for the distraction and on the other, she wasn't. She needed, not wanted, to find out more about this guy. She had to take a few deep breaths to calm herself. These regulars didn't miss a thing and she didn't want them getting any ideas.

Another glance, another grin but no raise of the bottle. Lindsay made her way back down the bar to him. "Would you like another. Or is two your limit?"

"I'll take another. It's an easy day and I'm rather enjoying myself."

"At my expense. How sweet." Lindsay hated the thought that he could see what he did to her and did not miss the regulars eyeing him out of curiosity and wonderment. He didn't miss the glances his way or the whispers among the regulars. Hopefully, the crowd would die down and she could think of something to say to him to get him to talk instead of just teasing her.

Lindsay stayed busy, making her wonder if the regulars were sticking around to figure the new guy out and any connection between him and her. As she walked by him on her way to deliver another drink, he said, "Hey pretty lady, could I get my tab please, when you have a minute?"

"It's too much trouble right now." She grinned at him and gave him a wink. The wink was to cover the new emotions of him calling her "pretty lady." What was this effect? She didn't like being this out of control and had never been this out of control of her own emotions.

On her next pass by, she gave him his total. "Thanks, Lindsay." But he didn't move to leave. This time she was determined to see him go and see what he drove. She was starting to think he was an angel that could appear and disappear. Him calling her by name. No, she wasn't liking the effects he had on her. She didn't know what to make of it.

While continuing to wait on others, her mind was on something to talk to him about. She was never speechless and could strike up a conversation with complete strangers. That's it! There was a concert tomorrow night. She would ask him if he was going. This way she would find out if he was still going to be in town, a new local or just a passerby. As she turned to ask him, he was gone. She didn't miss the instant disappointment she felt.

At least tomorrow was Friday and her last day of the week to work so she wouldn't have to wait all weekend to maybe see him again the following week. If he was still in town. That meant she was sure he would be back tomorrow.

26

Kendall was determined to go to Philadelphia to follow Jack from the airport. She didn't want to drive to the airport and wait around though and she didn't want to waste time.

"Hi, Jack. Just calling to check in since I haven't heard from you in a few weeks. Everything good?"

"Kendall, what a surprise. It's good to hear from you but please tell me you aren't bored already?"

"No, it's just strange not talking to you since I have at least a few times a week for the past few years. No jobs for me yet?" Kendall wondered what was really going on with no jobs available or at least none that Jack was putting her on.

"I thought we might give you a few months to regroup and enjoy yourself a little before the next battle round. You've been pushing hard the past few years."

"I see. I wasn't expecting a few months. You don't have a replacement for me, do you?"

Jack smirked at that thought. "That's the funniest thing you've ever said. You know you are invaluable to us."

Kendall wasn't so sure about that. "Glad to hear it, Jack. How about dinner tonight?"

"Sorry, Kendall. I'm flying out of town tonight. How about next week?"

"I don't know. I may be off in Aruba next week or maybe skiing in Colorado now that I know my vacation is for a few months."

"Kendall, you can't be bored."

"No, I actually picked up a fun little job to keep me busy and to get out and meet people. It's going well."

Jack was intrigued. "Do tell!"

"Sorry. I have to run. We'll catch up next week."

Hanging up the phone, she regretted telling him that. He would probably have someone follow her to see what she was doing. Let's hope she wasn't being followed. She would have to be more watchful.

At least now she suspected Jack would be arriving at the airport so it wouldn't be wasted time waiting around for him. Keeping busy was good for her.

Kendall drove to Philadelphia and even though she hit rush hour traffic, arrived just as Jack's helicopter landed. This perfect timing must be a sign that she was doing the right thing in trying to find out what was really going on and who the boss is.

She drove out of the parking lot and up the street so that she wouldn't be following Jack from the moment he got in his car. Luckily, there was a long road out of the airport with other buildings and businesses. Kendall pulled into a parking lot at the end of the road for good measure. Less time she would be following him. Several cars had driven by but not Jack's Mercedes.

When Jack failed to drive by within fifteen minutes, Kendall drove back to the airport. His Mercedes was still there. What was he doing inside? She would just have to wait here.

After two hours of waiting, Kendall was beyond frustrated. Following people wasn't usually in her job description and Jack knew she couldn't, or wouldn't, sit still to wait someone out.

She saw him get out of the helicopter so she knew he was there. What was he doing inside? Even if she had put on the wig she wore last time she went into the airport, Jack more than likely would recognize her.

Kendall had two choices, continue to wait in her car or get out and go look for him. The latter was a higher risk but Kendall wasn't one to wait around. She had checked out the cameras and had already figured out hidden areas and blind spots. She was thankful for the cover of darkness and her black clothing.

She eased out of her car and was thankful she was driving the black nondescript Accord that had the fake registration. Jack didn't miss much and no doubt knew all, or most, of the cars in the parking lot. She jogged over to the front side of the reception building. She moved along the front towards the front door. Once there, and after checking her surroundings, she took out a visual scope attached to a very thin but very long pole and placed it just past the edge of the door, low to the ground to see inside. Kendall wasn't sure if it was good or bad that no one was there.

She moved back towards the side of the building. With only four hangers this shouldn't take long, provided she didn't get caught.

The first two hangers were empty and silent. Approaching the third hanger, Kendall had a feeling this one wasn't empty. She loved and valued her gut. It saved her more times than she could count. Using extra caution, she stood completely still against the wall and waited, listening intently. Shortly, a security guard came running out the door, headed back to the reception building. She silently exhaled as she waited two more minutes, hoping she hadn't triggered an alarm somewhere. Nothing. She pulled the visual scope out again and placed it in front of the side door window. No one.

Instead of going in, she circled to the opposite side of the hanger, putting her further away from the reception building and her car. There were windows high up on the side of the wall. She could climb it with her gear but had left it in the car and climbing metal would mean that she would have to be able to latch onto something. Throwing the hook into the window frame was too risky. She didn't want to accidentally break the window. She pulled out the visual scope, checked her surroundings again and lifted the scope to one of the windows.

Inside were two men in plain sight discussing

something. She should have put the microphone on the extender also. No time. She was looking for Jack, not two strange men. Moving the scope angle, she didn't see anyone else. Watching for a few more minutes didn't reveal anyone else in the hanger.

Kendall jogged over to the last hanger. Hanger four was like the first two. Empty. Where was Jack?

Stopping back by hanger three, there was still no sign of Jack. Where was he? She would have to check inside the reception building.

Quickly and quietly, she moved to the back of the reception building cautiously avoiding the security camera's vision. Unless someone was literally sitting there watching, they wouldn't see her in the darkness and she doubted the cameras have heat sensors. She would have to hope for the best because she needed to get close to a window.

As she approached the closest window, she heard a small plane coming in for a landing. That meant anyone inside would be coming out to greet the plane.

Making her way quickly along the back of the building and down the side, she arrived at the front of the building just as two men were approaching the front door. Neither was Jack. She could tell one of them was quite tall and very well built. Bodyguard type. This was good and bad. Good in that whoever was on that plane was important. Bad in that whoever was on that plane was important and security would be on alert.

Kendall decided not to risk going inside but instead waited near the front corner of the building until security had checked down the side. Using her scope, she watched and she waited. Once the guard had checked down the side and moved on, she made her way along the side again. There were three windows into which she could glance and see most of the interior.

No Jack. Where was he? She made her way back to her car. Sitting there for a moment, she replayed the last few hours in her mind. She knew she had seen Jack get out of the helicopter and she knew his Mercedes was still in the parking lot. He was not here unless he was tucked into an office she hadn't seen. She doubted that. Jack wasn't one to sit still very long.

Kendall wasn't one to sit still very long either and wasn't disappointed when the two men didn't make her wait long before coming out of the airport. Two other men had joined the bodyguard and his cohort. One was a gentleman of average build and nondescript and the other, a tall, dark and very handsome man. She could tell he was more handsome than most with just the little light from the street lamps, although she couldn't see his face clearly. But no Jack.

This wasn't odd. What was odd was that the four men got into Jack's Mercedes and drove off. She would follow now. How lucky could she get?

She followed them through the streets of Philadelphia for a few miles, staying at least one traffic light behind them. She knew the bodyguard was indeed a bodyguard and that whoever the men were from the plane, they were important, or dangerous.

They pulled into a parking garage. Kendall knew following them into that structure would not be wise.

They may have made her and if so, would be waiting. Parking garages were typically one way in and one way out and the last place one wanted to have a negative encounter. There were not a lot of escape routes. She would have to drive by and do more research.

Lindsay usually looked forward to Fridays at the bar. Fridays were her busiest day of the week and she had the weekends off. She enjoyed spending the weekends with her sons more so than ever. There was no stress and no taking work home from this job.

The visitation that the judge granted Brad was ridiculous and he continued to play games where the boys were concerned. Although she was supposed to pick them up at six every weekday, except Wednesdays when they stayed with their father, they would call and ask to stay later because Daddy was taking them to miniature golf, or the play center or had rented a movie. He was playing Disneyland Dad perfectly. Lindsay was supposed to have them every other weekend, but it changed all the time, depending on what Brad was doing and if he grabbed the boys Friday night. Of course, if Brad didn't have plans for the boys, Barbie did. Lindsay needed to find another attorney who would actually work. She needed to file a contempt charge against him for all the times he took the boys on her time.

This Friday was busy as usual but seemed to be in slow motion waiting on Mr. Gorgeous to show up. She wanted him to but she wanted him not to.

He was a no show. Lindsay was sad but felt it a relief in some ways. She still didn't like the ways in which he made her feel, physically and mentally. She shouldn't be looking forward to seeing him with no guarantee that she would. He could have been married with no ring or in a relationship with someone, or worse yet, a womanizer, like Brad. It was going to be a long weekend waiting for work on Monday to see if he showed again. She needed to stay busy and stop thinking about him so much.

That afternoon when the night/weekend bartender showed up to replace Lindsay, she asked her if she could by chance work Saturday. Lindsay found it disturbing that her first thought was yes, just in case Mr. Gorgeous showed up. Disturbing indeed. She had never fought herself like this.

"Sure. Is it usually busy?" Lindsay hoped it would be. She hated to be idle. Of course, she was also hopeful.

"It can be. They have added a second day of the rock concert because their show that was supposed to be tomorrow in another city got canceled."

"Wow, talk about the last minute."

"Not really. They have been announcing it for the past few weeks. Lindsay, you really need to get out more. Have fun tomorrow."

Brad had picked the boys up Friday even though it wasn't his weekend, again. This time he saved Lindsay from getting a sitter to watch them but she was still fuming.

Saturday started busier than the weekdays. The bar was almost packed at 10:30 am. Most were getting a head start on the concert. Lindsay happened to be at the end of the bar near the back door when what appeared to be a homeless man walked in like he owned the place. He took one of the few remaining open seats at the bar, put his stuff down and told Lindsay, "Get me a beer."

"Any particular kind or my choice?" Lindsay hated it when people just ordered a "beer." It was like pulling teeth to figure out which one they wanted. Beer drinkers were typically picky. To Lindsay, they all were the same since she wasn't a beer drinker. Although, when Mr. Gorgeous ordered a beer, Lindsay hadn't even thought about how much she hated it.

"Draft."

"Regular or light?"

"Lady, I don't care. I'm thirsty."

Lindsay was relieved at the draft request since it was the cheapest and she was worried the homeless appearing man was going to stiff her.

"There you go. Regular. That's $2.25 please."

"Start me a tab."

That was the last thing Lindsay wanted to do and he picked up on it pretty quickly by the eyebrow raise when Lindsay just looked at him.

"I'm good for it. I promise, I won't stiff you."

Lindsay must have been obvious with her expression.

Most people had no idea what she was thinking. It was a little early for this. Lindsay needed more coffee and fewer arrogant homeless guys.

Lindsay continued doing her job when the homeless guy said, "Hey pretty, set the bar up and get me another."

Lindsay looked around the bar, took a quick inventory of how much that would cost and told him, "That's going to be $154."

"Fine, whatever. I didn't ask. Just do it. And don't tell them who it's from."

He was definitely stiffing Lindsay but something inside her made her do anyway.

As Lindsay was setting the bar up with their drinks, the bar owner sat down and looked at her with a questioning look.

"Don't ask. And hope he doesn't stiff me." Her boss just grinned. Her boss knew Lindsay would be watching the guy and he wasn't likely to get far off his barstool before Lindsay was all over him. People tried to stiff her but she had no problem calling them out, loudly to be sure everyone heard and looked at them. That little trick usually embarrassed them and they couldn't get their money out fast enough.

In under ten minutes, the homeless guy asked her to set the bar up a second time. Lindsay had to put her foot down and demand he pay up. He just looked at her like he was bored and put a stack of money on the bar. "Don't take it now. Keep a tab. I'll pay you, sweets. This is pennies."

After Lindsay gave him his beer, he asked where her

boss was and she pointed to him at the other end of the bar. He got off his barstool, leaving the pile of cash there, and walked over to the boss while Lindsay was setting the bar up again.

As the homeless guy walked towards him, Lindsay's boss looked at her with that "Here we go" look. "That's the best bartender I've ever seen. I've seen bartenders in every state and hundreds, no thousands, of bartenders. She's great with customers but protective of you and this bar at the same time. Man, that's hard to find. She's a gem. And not hard on the eyes either." The boss just grinned and said, "I know it."

After the homeless guy bought two more rounds for the entire bar, he asked Lindsay for his tab. When Lindsay gave him his total, he didn't bat an eye, threw several hundred-dollar bills at her and told her to keep the change. As he got up off his bar stool, he told her it was time for him to move on before they found him. After finding some hundred-dollar bills stuck together, Lindsay told him it was way too much. He told her to buy herself something pretty.

That was probably the craziest paying customer Lindsay had ever had and it made her wonder who he was and what his story was. Her tip was bigger than his bar tab, even after setting the bar up four times.

After he left, the customers were trying to figure him out. About ten minutes later, Ben came running through the door. "Hey Lindsay, was there a homeless-looking guy in here today?"

"Yes. Friend of yours?" Lindsay was half teasing. Ben knew a lot of people from different walks of life.

"The lead singer for the band tonight. The whole band has been out drinking all night and I was able to round all of them up except him."

"Wait, what? Wow! I can't believe he was the lead singer of that internationally known band. I got to meet him, sort of. He did say I was the best bartender he ever met out of thousands." As Lindsay reflected on this morning, Ben brought her back to attention quickly.

"Lindsay! I'll get you back stage passes. Which way did he go?" Ben hadn't stopped moving from the back door through the bar to the front door. Lindsay pointed towards the front door and off Ben went. He was head of security at the arena where the band was playing.

This was a nice morning distraction and kept Lindsay's mind off Mr. Gorgeous. About noon, he walked through the back door with another man. Maybe Mr. Gorgeous and this guy were band groupies or stagehands. That would explain the sudden appearance of him this week.

"Hey, pretty lady! Good to see you here. I didn't think you worked weekends." Lindsay wondered why he thought that. She hadn't told him. Of course, they hadn't really talked about anything at all except beer and tabs.

"Hey, you. I would say hey your name but I don't know it. I usually don't work weekends but the other bartender needed the day off." There was that shaking again. Breathe. Lindsay breathe.

"Well, where have my manners been? I'm Sam Stone and this is my cousin and friend, Tim Stone." He reached across the bar to shake Lindsay's hand and that was it. She was completely done in. She knew he had to feel that. It was like a lightning bolt. It literally jarred her and made her catch her breath. Tim noticed and had started to put out his hand to shake her hand as well, but withdrew it quickly to save Lindsay from having to stay any longer. Lindsay thought her heart was going to beat out of her chest. She had to get away from him quickly.

"Two of the same?" she asked as she turned and started to walk away.

"No, Tim doesn't have as good a taste in beer as I do. Get him a regular draft please and I'll take a Bud." If Sam had noticed or felt anything, he gave no indication and didn't miss a beat. Had Lindsay been looking at him and not Tim, she would have seen something in his eyes change, but that was it.

"You've got it." She got the Bud first and put it in front of him. She didn't think she could get the draft to Tim without spilling it. That handshake shook her to her core. She prayed to God above to let her put the mug in front of Tim without spilling it and making a complete fool of herself. No such luck. "Hold on. I'll get a rag." As Lindsay headed towards the sink at the other end of the bar, she tried to pull herself together. What had happened to the calm, cool, collected, and strong Lindsay Phillips? She was nowhere to be found in the presence of this one. She hated chaos and this guy seemed to bring out mental chaos in her.

As she started to wipe the spilled beer on the bar in front of Tim, Sam put his hand on hers and said, "I've got it." He had to have felt that one! What was going on with him, with her? She was kind of sorry he came in.

She tried staying away from him the rest of the afternoon but apparently, the more he drank the more he liked to talk. He was having a good time with Tim and smiling and laughing entirely too much for Lindsay's peace of mind. The grin did her in but the smile and laugh were close.

"Hey Lindsay, can you be the tiebreaker for us, please?" Sam was polite and had manners as well as being drop-dead gorgeous. He had to be an angel.

"Sure, what's up?"

"Tim says you are happily married. I say you are not."

"Was the absence of a ring your first clue?" She winked at him and wanted to ask him if it mattered with the chemistry between them but thought better of it.

Tim in his own defense, "But lots of bartenders don't wear rings because it could hurt their tips or they catch them on the bottles. So that doesn't really tell anything."

Lindsay didn't answer. She grinned and walked off. Let him stew about it and see how much it mattered. She would know by how long it took him to respond.

When Sam had gone to the bathroom, Lindsay went to check on Tim hoping he might give something up. She found it easier to talk to Tim. "Are you guys local or here for the concert or work?" Before he could answer, she got called away. Walking away, she told Tim to "Hold one."

When she came back, Sam answered, "We're locals. Well, I just moved here but Tim's been here for a few years." So, they were talking about her.

"How nice. Where did you move here from?"

"Down the street." Grin induced.

"That would still make you a local. Nice way of telling me it's none of my business?" She had a grin of her own.

They bantered back and forth the rest of the afternoon. She was a hot mess with him so close to her most of the day. Lindsay wasn't sure if she wanted the day to last forever or to end quickly.

The night bartender made her appearance and that signaled all the customers to close out or tip. She stayed away from Sam and Tim's end of the bar until they were the last customers for her.

Sam said, "I guess it's that time of day for you to head out pretty lady. Can you get our tab, please? One tab is good. I've got this."

"You don't have to close out."

"It's okay, we've been here longer than planned anyway." This could be a good sign. Lindsay chastised herself for thinking she had anything to do with that. She did find out he was single once she finally told him she was happily divorced. You know men though; didn't mean he was.

Lindsay was trying to take her time in leaving by standing on the opposite side of the room but still behind the bar. She was by the front door and they had come in the back. Sam and Tim made their way around the bar to the front where Lindsay was. Tim went out the door but Sam walked behind the bar and stood within inches of her. Lindsay felt like she was standing outside of herself, watching a movie and holding her breath. She didn't know what to make of this at all. It was an experience she had never had.

In a very southern drawl, Sam said, "Hey pretty lady, I would never be so presumptuous as to ask for your telephone number but if you would like to get together outside of here, here is my number. I would be ever so delighted." He put the paper on the counter in front of them. Lindsay was glad she didn't have to reach for it because she wasn't sure she could move with him this close.

Lindsay thought of only grinning and not responding but she didn't want to play games and leave him guessing. In her best southern accent, "Then I shall delight you." As soon as it was out of her mouth, she blushed. No one had ever made her blush and this was the second time he did. Or rather, she made herself in front of him for being so dumb. Losing the southern accent, Lindsay responded, "I would very much like to see you outside of here."

Sam gave her the biggest smile she had seen yet and said, in almost a whisper, "I shall very much look forward to it." With that grin and a wink, he was gone.

28

K endall couldn't find anything related to PJ
Enterprises located in the office building the four
men in Jack's Mercedes had pulled into the other night.
There were no investigation companies in that office
building. She had even called the information desk to
ask. Nothing.

Dead ends. She didn't like them. She didn't want to
keep driving to Philadelphia either. Waiting around for
Jack's helicopter, or rather PJ Enterprise's helicopter, to
come and go was time-consuming. Kendall was still
bewildered as to where Jack went after he landed.

She played with the idea of going to dinner with
Jack and keeping the conversation personal. Kendall
didn't know much about Jack now that she thought
about it. He was well trained, had more experience than
her and would find her curiosity about anything
personal involving him cause for alarm. He had seemed
to share more with her when they were younger. They
used to talk for hours when she was a teenager.

Remembering back, what they mostly talked about was her. What she wanted to do, what she thought, how school was going. Back then, Jack was easy going, fun and intriguing. But still, whenever she brought up meeting the boss, he would get frustrated and close down.

Kendall's next thought was of seducing Jack. She didn't see that going well because he would take her to her place or a hotel. If he lived in Philadelphia, he certainly wouldn't take the time to fly her there. If she were to pretend drunk, there were too many places closer. Unless he didn't live in Philadelphia. Then what was the connection that Jack flew in and out of there so often? He had to live there. Somewhere.

Having no other options that she could see, Monday morning she was at the Philadelphia private airport at 6 a.m. waiting for Jack. His Mercedes wasn't there so at least she hadn't missed him.

At 7:30 a.m., a black Camry with tinted windows pulled in to the parking lot. No one got out for a few minutes and Kendall was thinking it was probably an employee since it was a Camry. Kendall almost went back to her research on her laptop when the door opened and Jack got out. This is how she missed him. He had more than one car. Why?

Kendall stayed in her car until Jack got into the helicopter and flew off. She drove past the Camry and got the license plate number and took a mental picture of the Camry.

Kendall ran the license plate. It came back registered to a company named Elle, Inc. "L" as in Langston? She then pulled up the Directory for the parking garage into which Jack's Mercedes had driven. Elle, Inc. Suite 107B. This meant two things. One, the guys she had followed before probably hadn't made her and two, suites starting with 1 were on the first floor. She could pull the fire station logs to check their security system. The fire station would have done inspections every six months and noted any alarm systems in the event of a fire.

No special alarms were noted by the fire department. Since she was dressed in running gear and was in the city, now would be a good time to check out the building. It was Monday so there would be people around and possibly in the office. She could check out the public areas of the building and the outside then figure out the best way to get in the office.

The office building was one of the more elaborate buildings in the area of Cranston Avenue. Philadelphia was known for its rich, long history and many buildings dated back to the 1800s. This one was not as old, but certainly not as modern as some. Kendall was glad it was older. This meant most companies in the building weren't as concerned with high tech security systems. It was also located in the business district which typically had low crime.

Entering the lobby, she was able to slip past the information desk without notice. She walked down the first hallway, locating the door to Suite 107B. Peeking in the window next to the door, she didn't see anyone. It was a split-second decision and she knew Jack wasn't there.

"Hello?" Silence. A second call out. Nothing. She

walked behind the reception area to a hallway and took a casual stroll down, calling out "hello" every few steps. She was able to take in an office on either side of the hallway. One had a conference table and chairs and the other was filled with filing cabinets. At the end of the long hallway, there was a closed door. Kendall approached the door cautiously. She listened for a moment and hearing nothing, she knocked and called out. Silence. Trying the handle, the door opened.

Kendall scanned the office quickly. No one was here. The office was filled with beautiful furniture. To her left, there were wall to wall wood shelves of obvious high quality. In front of those was a sitting area with beautiful floral furniture. The opposite side of the office was another wall full of beautiful wood shelves filled with expensive art sculptures and in front of those a fully functioning, large, wood desk and a picture of her. She quickly glanced around the entire office, memorizing it for later, then bolted out.

Reaching the end of the hallway to the reception area, she bumped into a very attractive, older lady.

"Oh, I'm so sorry. There was no one out here when I came in and I think I'm on the wrong floor. I need the Chiropractor in Suite 207. So sorry." Kendall had said most of that while heading towards the exit door so the lady couldn't get a good look at her face. Under a plain, black baseball hat, her wig was deep red so she wasn't worried about the lady recognizing her. Hopefully, the southern drawl would help her disguise as well.

Kendall jogged back to her car four blocks away. She wanted to avoid parking garages. As she jogged, she took in every face in case she recognized anyone. Getting in her car and catching her breath, she replayed the office through her memory. She gasped as she realized there had been two more pictures of her. They were on the shelves beside the desk among the sculptures. One was her when she was fifteen and the other was her when she was about twenty-five. The photo on the desk was within the last few years.

Whose office was this? Not Jack's. Why would he have pictures of her? If not Jack, then who?

29

Lindsay was still walking on Cloud 9 after Sam gave her his number. Should she wait to call him? No, she never played games and always went after what she wanted. Did she want her life tilted upside down, or at least, over as she knew it? It was too late. It was already over. It was over the moment she saw him for the very first time, sitting there with that grin. She wanted to see where this would go and she might as well spend time with him instead of just having him on her mind. All the time. It was Sunday and she was unexpectedly open since Brad had the boys, again.

She almost hung up after the first ring, but he answered.

"Hey, Sam. It's Lindsay."

She was surprised at Sam's answer, "Hi, pretty lady! I wasn't sure I would hear from you."

"You knew you would. There is a Blues Festival down by the water. I was thinking of going. Care to join me? I know it's short notice."

"I would love to if you don't mind picking me up. Car issues right now."

"That's fine. Text me the address. Half an hour?" That may explain why she never saw him come or go from the bar. He was walking. She still should have seen him walking away though. Or coming through the door.

From the moment she laid eyes on him waiting by the entrance to the gated community, she started shaking and her heart started racing. She was going to have to start taking Valium if she didn't get herself together every time she saw him. Maybe this would be good for her. Maybe he would turn out to be a jerk.

They enjoyed the day walking around the Blues Festival listening to music and walking along the boardwalk by the water, just talking and getting to know each other. He really was a great listener. He once put his hand on her arm and slid his other arm around her to move behind her when another couple with young children took up most of the boardwalk. Lindsay did not know how she didn't ignite right then with every nerve in her body sending electrical currents through her whole nervous system. When he took her hand to hold it as they were walking, it jolted her insides although it felt like the most natural thing in the world. She immediately turned to him. He was grinning that grin and said, "It this okay?" Just like he didn't feel a thing.

Lindsay had to know, "Has that ever happened to you before?"

"No." He didn't have to ask her what she was talking about. Then, "What is your favorite food."

And just like that, the subject was closed and he

casually moved on. At least one of them could remain level headed.

They finished off the date at a local favorite restaurant by the water, talking for hours and only leaving when it got crowded and too loud to talk.

When Lindsay dropped Sam off, he insisted the gated area was fine. He could walk to the house. She asked, "Are you sure you aren't married or have a significant other?"

"Yes, I'm sure. It's faster for me to walk from here than it is for you to drive and get turned back around."

"Trying to hurry away?" She chuckled.

He was very serious. "I had the best time I've had in years with you today, Lindsay. I'm working out of town all week but I may stop in at the bar if that changes. If that's okay with you?"

"Yes, and you have my number from when I called you. Thank you for today. I had a great time as well. Have a good week."

He barely breathed "thank you," grinned, got out of the passenger seat and walked away. She was glad he hadn't kissed her. She may have exploded, been blinded or dropped dead. Shaking her head, she asked herself, "What am I? Fifteen again?"

K endall was filled with dread when she saw that Jack was calling this early. He couldn't know she was checking him out. She had been extremely careful.

"Kendall! Hey, let's do that dinner this week. When is good for you?"

"I don't know, Jack. I have a crazy week coming up."

Kendall was still processing the drastic changes in her life as of late. One thing at a time would have been enough. She so wanted to blurt out, "Who's Elle, Inc. and why do they have pictures of me in their office?" She was no closer to figuring things out than she was when she was in their office.

"Are you okay? You don't sound like yourself?

Kendall would have to be very careful during this conversation. "Yes, I've only been awake for a few minutes really. Still waiting on coffee to brew."

"I've talked to you in the mornings, remember? This isn't you. Are you sure you are okay?"

"Yes. Maybe I'm a little tired. Let me check my schedule this week. What do you have open?"

"I have Wednesday open. I know those are usually easiest for you."

"Yup. Let's do Wednesday. I'll make it happen. Thanks, Jack."

"I look forward to seeing you, Kendall."

He's never said that before. Her imagination was in overdrive. Damn him for knowing her so well and picking up on a change in her. This was going to be more difficult than she initially thought. If Jack thought something was wrong with her, he would be watching her. She needed to get it together.

Kendall wasn't completely coming apart. She could still think on her feet. Brilliant move agreeing to dinner with Jack on Wednesday. She would cancel at the last minute. He would then just go home since he wouldn't have time to make other plans. Kendall would be waiting in Philadelphia.

All week Lindsay was in her own little world at the bar but still able to lay them out with her famous one-liners and wittiness. Customers noticed she was overly happy and nothing seemed to bother her.

"So, is this the new and improved dating Lindsay?" from the same customer, the one she called "Drama Llama", who wanted to intervene last week but ended in surrender.

"Funny guy. What's for lunch?"

"You seriously have a sparkle in your eye! I can't believe it! You went out with him, didn't you? I want to hear all about it. What's his name?"

"You are worse than a woman! Drama Llama. His name is Sam."

"Oh, I will be needing more details than that. I've never seen you this happy!"

And that's how it went all week. Drama Llama was the only one to pick up on why Lindsay was a little distracted. Others tried to get information and guessed she had met someone new but didn't know who. Their guesses were entertaining.

Lindsay didn't hear from Sam until he appeared at the bar late Friday afternoon. Lindsay came back from the kitchen, and there he was, just like he had been there all day. How did he do that? Did he plan it? She would have to discuss this with him later.

"Hi, pretty lady. Could I get a Bud please?" Just like he was a regular and didn't know her outside of the bar.

"Sure. Eating today?"

He leaned forward and whispered, "Only if you will go somewhere with me when you get off work?" There was that grin because he already knew she wouldn't say no.

"I'm sorry, I can't. I have other plans." The disappointment was quick as a flash before he replaced it and said, "That's too bad. I was really looking forward to spending more time with you."

Lindsay had a grin of her own and said, "I would love to have dinner with you tonight. Please figure out where you want to go because I'm starving now and don't want to try to figure it out when I get off in a half-hour." She saw that sparkle return to his eyes and his lips mouthed "Thank you." Gorgeous, a great listener, considerate, well mannered. She didn't know if she should be thrilled or find the fault.

For the next several weeks, that's how it went. Lindsay didn't hear from Sam during the week but saw him on the weekends when the boys weren't around. She didn't want them to meet unless things got serious. Drama Llama came in every day to keep updated.

One Tuesday, Lindsay was having a hard day, which she rarely did. She was surprised when her phone rang that afternoon and it was Sam.

"Hey, babe. How are you?"

"Hi, Sam. I'm fine. You? Is everything okay? It's Tuesday."

"I can tell everything is not fine. What's wrong pretty lady?"

Lindsay wasn't sure how he knew her so well. He could tell just from the sound of her voice? "Just a bad day. It will be fine later."

"Anything I can do? How about if I come over tonight after work?"

"Really? I would love that!"

"Okay, I'll see you tonight. If for some reason, anything changes, I will call you and let you know."

"Perfect. See you tonight."

Drama Llama was sitting at the bar and when Lindsay turned around from that call, he was smiling from ear to ear. "You know Lindsay, I'm really happy for you. Man, I've never imagined I would see you so happy. It's so cool. You guys seem to really have something."

Lindsay didn't say anything and just rolled her eyes as if he was being dramatic. Then she couldn't help herself, "He scares me. I mean really scares me. I've never felt this way and no one has ever had this effect on me. I'm not sure if he is real. I mean, I hope he is who he says he is."

"C'mon Lindsay, who else could he be and why would he not be legit."

She couldn't, or wouldn't, answer that.

3 2

Kendall was glad Jack couldn't tell when she was lying. She didn't do it to Jack often, but it seemed more and more lately, she was.

"Jack! I'm glad I caught you. I'm so sorry, I got stuck where I am and can't leave right now. I can't make dinner. I'm sorry."

"Are you okay, Kendall? I can come to get you."

"No, it's nothing like that. I'm just helping someone with something and there's a deadline and we may not make it. I didn't realize how late it was getting. Can we reschedule?"

"Sure, Kendall. And hey, you still don't sound right. Are you sure you are okay? Talk to me. Let me help if I can."

"Jack, I promise you, I'm fine. Really."

She would love his help. Asking Jack to answer a few questions though would not get her what she wanted. Answers. She would get them without him. Or rather, in

143

spite of him. She was already sitting at the airport in Philadelphia.

Kendall wouldn't make the mistake of driving to the end of the street to wait for Jack like she had the last time. She drove to the first set of office buildings after leaving the airport parking lot. Here she could park and see the airport. She had her binoculars. It would be less obvious following Jack out of here.

Jack's helicopter landed in just about the timeframe Kendall figured. Jack exited the building and although his Mercedes was in the parking lot, he jumped into a white SUV. How fortunate for Kendall. He would be easier to follow in this.

As Jack pulled out of the airport parking and drove past her, she waited about 30 seconds, then followed behind him, always keeping a safe distance.

She followed Jack around the edge of the city on a major highway. Rush hour was about over so traffic was perfect for following but not too closely.

He went from the fast lane to the slow lane in a quick maneuver. Kendall hoped this was just Jack's bad driving and not that Jack made her. She had been in the middle lane so it wasn't as obvious when she slowly made her way over to the slow lane, then followed him off the exit.

They were now on a two-lane road, passing middle-class neighborhoods. Kendall tried thinking back through conversations with Jack. He had never told her where he lived and she had never asked.

Jack put his signal on and made a left into a nice

neighborhood. She made a mental note of the street name, Ainslie Street. Kendall had no choice but to keep going. She pulled into the convenience store on the next corner and parked.

She jumped out and started her run back to Ainslie Street. She was thankful she had decided on the black running outfit and sneakers. She had on her hat with the brown wig and wouldn't be easy to recognize, even by Jack. He had never seen this disguise. Most of the wigs Jack had seen her wear didn't include hats.

As she came to the end of Ainslie Street, she caught the SUV making a turn onto another street at what looked like the last street in the neighborhood. She stepped up her run to the next street, Cheney Street, and was just in time to see the SUV pull into the garage of a house near the end of Langston Drive.

She rather liked this upper-middle-class neighborhood. Some of the yards had fences, but most didn't. They had hedgerows or small trees. It kept the neighborhood more open and made it appear larger than it actually was. All the homes had at least two-car garages and were neutral colors, even the shutters. Most had front porches and large decks. Some had stone with siding and others had brick with siding. Each yard was too big to push mow and only needed a small riding lawnmower. They probably hired landscapers and lawn care guys by the looks of the neighborhood.

Since dusk was closing in, she jogged up the opposite side of Langston Drive just as the garage door hit the pavement. She couldn't tell if there was another car in the garage. Several lights were on in the house but the blinds were closed. Kendall stored the house number into her photographic memory for later.

This house backed to the woods, not another house. Kendall jogged to the end of Langston Drive, making sure no one else was around, she jogged across the street and along the edge of the last house's yard and back into the woods.

She made it to the back of Jack's house, or at least the one where he pulled into the garage. Staying far enough in the woods not to be noticed, she pulled out her binoculars. Nothing to see. All the blinds were closed. It was now dark.

Just as she was trying to decide if she dared get closer, the lights over the deck came on, the blinds leading to the deck were pulled open and the sliders leading onto the deck opened. Jack and a dog came out. This yard wasn't fenced. She was a decent distance back in the woods. She held perfectly still, barely breathing.

The dog ran to the edge of the yard, barking ferociously. Just then Jack went back inside and Kendall took off running the opposite direction of the house, deeper into the woods. She saw the floodlights light up behind her but the dog didn't follow. Kendall figured there must be an invisible fence or he was extremely well trained. She heard Jack shout, "Killer! Stay!" She knew Jack couldn't see her this far back unless he was using a scope. Night vision wouldn't help at this distance. The dog's name must be Killer. How creative Jack.

Kendall realized the shortest distance back to her car was to go through the woods instead of back through the neighborhood. She hated the woods and more so in the dark. It would be best in this case. She was dealing with Jack after all. She made it back to her car at the convenience store, then jumped in and drove away as fast as she could legally go.

3 3

Lindsay wasn't her usual happy, sarcastic and witty self that week at the bar. Some of the customers noticed and some asked if she were ok. "Fine as frog hair" was her typical comeback. She really needed to get herself in check. She had never been moody, always the same good mood, sarcastic Lindsay, until recently. She realized she was extremely up and down emotionally since Sam had come into her life. She was either really happy and up or really sad and down. This was completely foreign to Lindsay. She wasn't one to let anyone else affect her mentally. Not even Brad could do that.

It wasn't until the next week Drama Llama came in. "Where have you been?"

"Aww did you miss me?"

"No, but when I needed a friend, you were a no show. Are you cheating on me, eating somewhere else?" Lindsay didn't tell many of the customers her business, but Drama Llama, whose real name was David

Dempsey, was one that she did. Mostly, because he didn't miss a thing and wasn't friends with others in the bar. Lindsay had met David several years prior when she needed a favor. At first, David wasn't agreeable to the favor. He came around after Lindsay held a knife to his throat and threatened him. He had taken her serious and granted her the favor. Lindsay then tested him and he proved his loyalty. He never approached her and never let on that they knew each other. He happened into the bar one day and ever since only acted like he knew Lindsay from the bar. He knew better than to ever let on to anyone that there was more to their story.

"I'll never tell. How is Sam? What do you need a friend for?" Drama Llama leaned closer over the bar as if their conversation was top secret.

"I don't. Just kidding since I usually see you every day." Lindsay knew the minute she said she needed a friend, it was a slip-up and regretted it, but was quick to recover.

"I think you missed me. I would hope you have been too busy with Mr. Wonderful to notice my absence. How is he by the way. Last time I was in, he was going over to your house, in the middle of the week."

"I have no idea."

"What do you mean? He showed up that Tuesday, right?"

"Nope. No show, no call. Lots of nothing."

"Did you call him? You guys had something special and were doing great."

"No, I didn't call him. I just feel like there's

something going on with him. Something he has to work through. He'll be back."

"Lindsay, what if he was in a motorcycle accident? Or hurt on the job. Or something."

"Then I would hope Tim would call me and let me know. I just have a feeling he needs space. For the first time in my life, I'm ok with someone ghosting."

"You must really like this guy because the Lindsay I know would never put up with this. I'm so sorry. I hope you are right and he comes back soon. No indication of what is going on with him? His history? Are you sure he's not married?"

"I've already asked myself all of the questions you can think of. No idea. I'm just comfortable in knowing that whatever he is dealing with, he'll be back. Eventually. Maybe at gunpoint, but whatever." Lindsay grinned at him to take the concern off and moved down the bar to wait on other customers.

34

Kendall was sitting by the window at the coffee shop staring blindly out when a familiar voice said, "May I sit?"

Kendall had been deep in thought and didn't see or hear Jack approach her. She was slipping. She knew better than to daydream or let herself mentally wander off in a public place. There was so much going on in her mind and she hated feeling like she wasn't making progress or in control. It seemed lately everything in her life was going in circles. Nothing was making sense and Jack being here sure as hell didn't make sense. "Jack. What are you doing on this side of town?"

"Looking for you. I've been worried about you and haven't heard from you lately. I was on my way to your house but stopped here for coffee. They have my favorite."

Kendall picked her phone up and checked it. She shook it at Jack. "Still works and you've never come to my house before. How often have you been in this coffee shop? What's going on? Got work for me finally?"

"Whoa! So many questions at once. I wanted to see you for myself and I need to talk to you about your next assignment if you are ready to come back to work. First things first. What's going on with you?"

"I'm not sure what you mean? I've been staying busy enjoying my time off. Reading a lot. Visiting new places. I may make visiting every coffee shop on the east coast my next venture. I'm fine, Jack."

"You were pretty lost in thought when I walked up. I haven't heard from you since you canceled dinner a few weeks ago."

"Just busy with…. busy and finding new things to do."

"Kendall, you can fool some of the people some of the time. You can never fool me. Not going to tell me about the new boyfriend?"

"How did you know about him? Seriously, are you following me or having me watched? If so, then you would know that was over as fast as it started."

Jack didn't miss the sadness in her eyes and thought to himself, "What do you know, Kendall Thomas has feelings after all."

"You know I keep tabs on you, Kendall. Protecting my asset. It was a lucky guess because I don't think we have ever gone this long without keeping in touch."

Kendall needed to change this subject and quickly. "I'm more than ready to get back to work. What am I doing and please don't tell me it's another long-term assignment? You know I like the short ones or the quick in and out."

"We have a few quick in and outs coming up. I know you prefer those." Commitments were hard for Kendall and Jack agreed the quick assignments were better for her. Less time for her to get ideas of her own.

"Perfect. Let me hear about it." They left the coffee shop and headed for Jack's car.

"We need you to go to Dallas next week. There have been lots of secret meetings and our client is not liking them. He's not a nervous guy but this has him way over the edge. We need to know where they are pulling money from and you will go in and see what you can find. This one is a little tricky. Top security. You will need to get into an office building and also a home office. You will need a partner to go in with you. No chance you want to take Tall One?"

"Is he still around? And no, I don't want to take Tall One."

"That's too bad. He asks about you often. Broke the poor guy's heart. I'll be in touch." With that, Jack waved her out of his car. She had barely gotten out when Jack drove off.

Kendall now had more to think about. She had been mentally reviewing all that she knew about Jack, Langston Corporation, Elle, PJ Enterprise and the house on Langston Drive. She hadn't followed Jack since the night she tailed him to the house with the dog on Langston Drive. She didn't miss the connection between Langston Corporation and the house on Langston Drive. She figured she would lie low for a bit. May have been a smart decision if Jack were having her watched. She had to ask herself, would Jack have her under surveillance? Something more to consider.

Her computer had been connected to the disposable phone when Jack joined her at the table. She didn't make a quick move to put it away as that would have drawn more attention to it. She was sure that Jack noticed it as he was very well trained. She was also sure that he wouldn't say anything to her but he would be checking things out with regards to it. He wouldn't find anything. Then again….

Kendall doubted Jack got lucky with a reference to the boyfriend. She was actually thinking about him in between thoughts of Jack and his companies. If Jack had been watching her, he would know that the boyfriend hasn't been around for a few weeks, much to her dismay.

35

L indsay had been doing well keeping busy but she did miss Sam every day. When she didn't have the boys, she was working extra. Part of her was hoping Sam would just appear again.

"Lindsay, I have to tell you something. I'm not sure how you are going to take this." Drama Llama didn't even wait until he was seated.

"If you know anything about Sam, don't tell me."

"No, it's actually not but this is really strange. I was getting my oil changed yesterday after work. I was walking around outside on the phone while I waited. This really tall guy walked up to me and told me to stay away from you or there would be trouble. Then he just walked off as if no big deal. How do you threaten someone then just walk off?"

"Blonde hair, skinny but well built? Jeans?"

"No, brown hair, about medium length, well built, cowboy hat and boots."

Lindsay thought for a moment. "Strange. I don't

know anyone that fits that description. He said that then just walked off? Did he work there or did you see what he drove?"

"No, partly because he disappeared around the corner of the oil place and partly because I was on the phone and bewildered. He was clean, no grease, so I assumed he didn't work there and I've never seen him before."

"What's even more strange, you are now the third person who has had this encounter. Same words, same description. One guy was at the bowling alley playing on his league and the other one had just walked into the jerk chicken place down the street. I wonder if that's what happened to Sam. I wonder if this guy threatened him too. You three are customers though you're here every day but Sam's not a customer and the most likely to be threatened."

"I think you should call him Lindsay. Would make sense and explain a lot. But I'm not sure why Sam wouldn't just tell you and try to figure out who he is and what his problem is."

"I'll call him."

"Now would be a good time. It's Friday afternoon. He should be back in town."

"There's a reason I call you Drama Llama. Let's see what he says." Lindsay wasn't so sure but what could it hurt. Sam was the most likely to be threatened although she didn't really see that scaring him off.

"Hurry up. I hope he did and that's why he ghosted."

Giving Drama Llama a look, Lindsay called Sam.

She was surprised he had answered. "Hey, Sam. It's Lindsay. Look, I hate to bother you but I was wondering if you have a second and can answer a question?"

"Well, that depends. You aren't bothering me but will the question bother me is the question?" She could hear the chuckle and knew he was teasing her. Her mind could also see the grin through the phone.

"It's not a personal question. Has a tall, brown-haired guy wearing a cowboy hat and boots threatened you in the last few weeks?"

"That question doesn't bother me and the answer is no. It's a strange question though. What's going on?"

"Three customers have told me that a guy fitting that description has threatened them. Basically, just telling them to stay away from me or there would be trouble. I don't know anyone who fits that description and I don't know why anyone would do that."

"Let's have dinner and see if I have the pleasure of his presence. I'll find out who he is and what his problem is."

"Dinner sounds good, but not a visit from him." Lindsay couldn't believe it. Dinner with Sam!

And just like that, things picked up between Lindsay and Sam as if they had never stopped.

K endall was ready for Dallas. She was hitting dead ends on researching Jack and had not dared to follow him since the dog incident and the coffee shop meeting.

The good news was that the boyfriend was back. She wouldn't tell Jack. She would wait and see if he mentioned him again. If he did, Kendall would know Jack was having her followed.

As she landed at the private airport outside of Dallas, Kendall caught sight of a really tall man wearing a cowboy hat and boots leaning up against the building. He was just standing there looking around like he had nothing better to do. He actually looked like a lost cowboy. He might be one of the new guys that had joined the organization since she had been out of the loop. But Jack hadn't mentioned anyone new and no one else was usually around when they flew in and out. Mostly for security reasons and because they didn't want to be seen.

As Kendall got off the airplane and walked toward the building, there was no else around. As she entered the reception area, she noticed the "lost cowboy" now sitting on a sofa reading a newspaper. His hat was off so she got a close look at him. She didn't say anything to him. If he was a new guy, he would either approach her or he would be getting into the SUV that was to take her to the meeting place. Maybe he was her driver. No, she knew Joe, who always drove them from the airports to the meeting place. Joe had been with the company for a long time and never missed a case. He could be trusted and was the best at not being followed. Jack hadn't said anything about meeting anyone at the airport. Maybe he was waiting on a flight out. Her mind was running wild these days and she was suspicious of everyone. She really needed to figure Jack and these companies out so she could stop the dramatics in her own mind.

Kendall didn't see anyone else and looking outside, she didn't see the SUV or Joe. Joe was never late. She headed into the ladies' room.

When she came out, Joe was looking around for her and the cowboy was gone.

"Hey, Joe. Good to see you. Did you see the tall guy with cowboy boots on out here when you came in?"

"No, Kendall. No one else has been through. This is Texas. Cowboy boots are as standard here as sneakers in most other states. Always good to see you. I've missed you."

"Thanks. Maybe I'm just being overly cautious." Kendall told Joe about the seemingly out of place cowboy.

"No. Let's go. I'll keep an eye out in case we are followed. Why do you suspect something's up, Kendall? Have you had any problems lately that I'm not aware of?" They got in the SUV and drove off. Joe scanned the parking lot and didn't see anyone.

"No, all is well. Just on high alert I guess with just coming back. No worries. I'm good."

A few miles down the road Joe whistled loudly. "Kendall, we are being followed. We'll lose him before we head over to the meeting place. It's not far but this will take a little longer. Sit tight."

"I guess you can't tell how tall he is and you didn't see the lost cowboy. What does he look like?"

"Brown hair, cowboy hat."

"You know you could hit a parking garage, see if he follows us in. Drop me off on one floor and I'll take the stairs up a level. Park there. And we'll wait for him."

"You got it Kendall but I wish you were driving and I could do your part. I know you got this."

"Block him in if he follows you up."

They turned into a parking garage with one way in and one way out. As Joe took the first turn, the car following them drove past the garage and didn't follow them in. "No go, Kendall."

"Shoot, I was up for a good fight and seeing who this guy is. I'll watch for the car on the way out. Are you sure he was following us?"

"Yes, I did a circle around the block back there before I mentioned it to you. Need to work out some frustrations or just excited to be back?"

"Excited to be back, Joe."

They made their way to the meeting place with no further incident. Kendall couldn't get this tall guy off her mind.

The crew welcomed her with lots of teasing about her extended vacation but were glad to have her back. She was glad to be back and trusted these people with her life. But not where Jack was concerned. She didn't trust anyone where Jack was concerned. The last thing she needed to do was start asking questions about Jack or the boss.

Kendall didn't give being followed another thought. She had a job to do. She was supposed to be in and out in under twelve minutes. It was three minutes in, eight minutes to find and review the documents and one minute out. The team sent in with her was well trained and she had worked with them on several other cases.

In under three minutes, the team got her in, along with another guy, Michael, she had worked with a few times. She and Michael found the documents she needed and had ample time to scan them into her memory. It was the one minute going out. Just as they started out, she was attacked from the side. The attackers came from behind a door that wasn't on the laboratory layout when she had reviewed it.

Not one but two. The first one got a perfect punch to Michael's throat, rendering him down for a minute. The second one got in a fistfight with Kendall. A perfect hit to the forehead knocked Kendall backward but gave her space to come back at him with a solid kick to his groin. She turned to see where Michael was along with the other assailant when she was grabbed from behind by Joe and dragged out the door. She had tried to go back in to see their faces but Michael was right behind her. He was putting his gun away as they started for the exit. Once they were back in the SUV, Kendall asked Michael if he had shot them. He had his silencer on so they wouldn't have heard the gunfire if he had. He said he hadn't because they were both down and his focus was on getting the team out without leaving dead bodies. Kendall would have shot both of them had she been given the chance. Or had fun kicking their asses first.

37

Lindsay settled into a comfortable pace at the bar and with Sam. The boys were doing great. Life was good.

Then life wasn't. One afternoon while Lindsay and Sam were sitting outside on the deck enjoying the day and each other, the front door burst open and Lindsay's oldest son burst through, crying hysterically and furious, red face and all.

"Hey, you! What's wrong? Calm down. It's okay."

He ran up to his room and Lindsay followed. "Mom, I'm never going back to Dad's. He won't stop embarrassing me in front of my friends. I have asked him to stop like you told me to but he won't. I can't take it. Even Aunty Barbie asked him to chill a little when we are there."

"Okay, okay. Calm down. Did he say why he won't stop?"

"No, just that it's his life and he is going to live it his way and do what he wants."

"Hey, bud. I'm sorry. You can't ignore it anymore, huh?"

"He's changed lately. His friends are strange. They go weird places. He hasn't told me where but I've heard him talking about them. I'm tired of all of his girlfriends being around. They all dress skimpy and it's gross. He's always touching them inappropriately, right in front of us and that's gross, too and embarrassing. He can do whatever he wants, but he's not going to do it around me anymore. I'm never going back there."

"Okay, let some time go by and we'll see what happens." Since Lindsay and Brad weren't on speaking terms, Lindsay didn't suggest to her son that she call his dad and talk to him. The best Lindsay could hope for right now was for her son not to have any lasting effects from Brad's behavior. Maybe if he stopped wanting to go over, Brad would realize he was an ass.

Lindsay left her son in his room and went back downstairs. "This isn't good."

"It didn't sound it. Dad still parading the women around?"

"Yep. Same stuff he has been complaining about. I don't get why Brad has to be such an ass. I don't really want to go back to court. No doubt Brad will turn this around and make it my fault. Although, you know we are in court every sixteen months about something. Guess we're due."

Maybe Sam couldn't handle the kid things or maybe he just didn't want to. Maybe he had other reasons, but the next week, he disappeared again. Gone like he never existed.

Lindsay didn't like it, but she had a feeling she should just let Sam walk away. Maybe it was the inner peace that told her he would be back. She was going to have to discuss this with him when he came back.

3 8

Kendall was happy with her first assignment in Dallas and completed it with the information she was after and then some.

Kendall was summoned to Jack's office upon her return. "Kendall! Great job in Dallas! How are the forehead and the rest of the body?"

"Thanks, Jack. It's great to be back and busy. The body has seen better days. It's all good."

"I heard about the suspicious guy that followed you and Joe. He's not one of ours and we are checking security cameras at the airport."

"Yes, it was strange. Too bad we didn't catch him when he was following us. No idea why? Do we have cameras at all of our airports?"

"Yes, we've had a few incidents a little while back. One of our clients was followed. There was someone sneaking around at one of the airports. We aren't sure if they are related. The one at the airport was small, not tall. No description since they were all in black from head to toe. We'll figure it out. Yes, all of the airports we fly into have cameras."

Kendall scanned her memory of the airport in Philadelphia. She was sure she had found and avoided all the cameras. She would replay that until she figured out where she was spotted. It was probably by the front window of the reception areas. And the "clients" did know that they were being followed. Glad her gut instinct kicked in and she didn't follow them into that parking garage. Had they figured out it was her she would have already known. She would definitely have to consider hiring someone. But who to trust?

"Jack, any idea what the two attackers wanted or why they were there?"

"No. We are looking into it."

"Jack, let me go back in. Maybe we missed something."

"Kendall, that information you obtained could either hurt several people or help them. Since we were there to be sure it didn't help them, I can only assume your attackers were there to help them. They were probably just thugs who got in right before you showed up."

"No, Jack. They wouldn't have heard us coming in time to "hide". And what was that door? There was a solid concrete wall where they appeared from and it wasn't on the floorplan I reviewed. They were coming in as we were leaving. I want to go back. They weren't thugs and you well know it."

"No way, Kendall. You were lucky you got out.

Those bruises are going to have you hurting for a while, too."

Kendall couldn't argue that.

Jack wanting to change this subject quickly, "Are you back with the boyfriend yet?"

"Why do you ask? Jack, you don't need to do a background check on everyone. Maybe I should and see if he wasn't hired by you." Kendall didn't miss the fact that Jack suspected they would end up back together. She may have to check him after all and hope he wasn't one of Jack's.

"I had thought about it, but not this time." Jack knew Kendall knew he was lying, or at the very least, not telling her the truth about something.

She wondered if she should mention the clients. No, she would let it go. Doubtful they are related. "Jack, please don't interfere with this one. I really like this guy. He's pretty special and not like anyone else. I want to see where this goes. As long as it's not interfering with my job, leave it alone. Please."

"Okay. But at the first sign of anything suspicious I will be on it."

"Where to next? I'm more excited to be back."

"We are thinking Mexico may be the next one. I'll be in touch."

Kendall was not going to let this go with finding out more about Jack and the boss, even though she just asked him not to do anything with the boyfriend. They were two different things. She was determined to find out the big secret. These incidences and the unknown cowboy were putting a strain on her ability to move about. They were watching.

Kendall was looking forward to seeing her boyfriend this weekend. She knew better than to get her hopes up though. But she had and he ghosted again. Gone like he never existed.

39

"Lindsay! Grab this order please!" She heard the bell. Relax. No one's food ever got cold around here. She was having a very busy day.

As she came back into the bar, she knew instantly something was off. Seconds later, a girl came running into the bar and punched a female customer in the face. The customer went flying onto the floor and the girl continued to punch her. Lindsay jumped over the bar and was on her before any of the other customers realized what was happening or could react. Lindsay grabbed the girl, putting both of the girl's hands behind her and so far up her back, she had no choice but to move any direction Lindsay moved her. Lindsay pushed her around the bar and right past the owner who came running when he heard the commotion. "I've got this." Lindsay opened the door and threw the girl out.

Lindsay went back behind the bar and back to work like nothing happened. Lindsay told the customers to watch the windows in case the girl came back in.

Lindsay served drinks to the waiting customers and was on her way back around the bar to collect the money or add them to their tab when the crazy girl came back in. Lindsay hollered to the girl she had attacked earlier but it was so loud, she didn't hear her. When one of the customers saw Lindsay starting to run towards that end of the bar where the last fight was, he stood up and blocked the crazy girl from getting by. Lindsay ran to the kitchen to get the owner and told the guy in the kitchen to call the police. "I've got work to do and she is bothering me."

Within minutes the police were there. Six of them filling out around the parking lot. As they came in the bar, Lindsay knowing all of them, gave them a wave and kept working like it was just another day. Lindsay's phone rang. She didn't usually check it when she was this busy but she happened to be passing by and saw that it was Sam. Snatching it up and continuing to work she answered, "Hey, you!"

"Lindsay, are you okay?"

"Why do you ask?"

"I am driving by and saw all of the police. What's going on? Are you okay?"

As much as Lindsay wanted to talk to Sam, it wasn't about this. "Yes, just a girl causing trouble. I'm good. Thanks for checking on me. I have to go. We're busy."

"Glad you are good. I was worried. Before you go, dinner tonight?"

"Sure. Text me where." Lindsay hung up without even a goodbye. He just happened to be driving by at the same time the cops were there? Lindsay was too busy to analyze Sam right now.

Shortly after the call, Sam came in. "I had to see for myself that you are okay. I was really scared for a minute."

"Is that your way of saying you miss me?"

"I do. And we need to talk. I'm sorry. I would like to talk with you."

40

Kendall was getting restless with everything going on. She didn't like herself when she got like this. She didn't like the unknown or being in limbo and lately, that's all she felt.

How was she going to work on finding out more about Jack and the boss? She was becoming obsessed with it. It seemed the less time she was able to devote to finding out, the worse she got. She just wanted answers once and for all.

Her boyfriend was back. She was going to have a talk with him about his disappearing and coming back. She would never have put up with this from anyone else. The thought that she was in love with him scared her. But there it was. She had never felt this way about anyone in her life. After all this time, he still affected her physically and mentally. She sometimes couldn't think about anything else for wondering what was going on with him and his disappearing acts. When left to think about it, she didn't like where her mind went. Was he also working for Jack? How much did he really know? He had never once given her any indication other than he was a regular guy, in all aspects of his life.

She knew he had been married and divorced. His ex-wife had alienated his children against him so he had no contact with them and it tore him apart inside. But he refused to do anything about it. He had been in the military for about ten years. In the last few years, he had roamed around in his grief of his ex-wife and his children. He wasn't still in love with his ex-wife. It was the grief of no contact with his children and all that she had done. He said he had worked for his uncle in a concrete business. They did the "pretties" on concrete architecture. Most of their business was in Washington, DC, and Philadelphia with the old buildings that needed restoration of the fancy scrollwork.

Philadelphia had registered with her when he said lots of their work was there. She had checked out his uncle's company and it was legit. It was owned by his uncle and his wife. Nothing had connected them to Jack or those businesses.

Kendall had suspected that he was one of those people who was afraid to get too close to anyone. He didn't believe he should have any goodness in his life because of his children. It was like self-imprisonment of his own mind and heart. He would sometimes intentionally ruin things if they were going well because he didn't believe he deserved them.

Kendall knew one thing. He had more belief in her than she did, and that was saying a lot because Kendall had full belief in herself from years of having no one else to depend on. There was Jack but she often wondered where he really stood and as of late, she didn't trust him much.

Her boyfriend treated her with nothing but respect, except the ghosting, but also with kindness, tenderness, admiration, and love. There it was. The four-letter word that scared her stiff. But he could put things in perspective as no one else had ever been able to. Not even Jack.

He was her best friend. Kendall could have deep, intense conversations with him. She had never had that either. He supported her in everything and was her biggest fan.

All so sad because it seemed no matter what Kendall did, she couldn't do the same for him. Even though he knew what she did for a living, it didn't appear to bother him because he had so much faith in her.

If only he would quit disappearing. She trusted him with almost everything, including her heart. The one thing she was not sure she could trust him with was Jack and the boss.

Kendall pretty much thought he walked on water. She would have to talk to him. A real sit-down, heart to heart.

41

"Lindsay, I need to have a heart to heart talk with you. Let's enjoy dinner first then we'll talk in private. Are you okay with that?" Sam knew she would be. Maybe she was too easy for him. Or maybe he felt the same connection and knew in the end everything would be okay.

"Sure. I'm starving and you know me, I can't focus on an empty stomach."

After dinner, they decided to go back to Lindsay's. Just as they were pulling in to her neighborhood, Lindsay noticed a tall guy walking out from the side of her house. He was wearing cowboy boots and a cowboy hat. Was that him?

"Sam, slow down! Look!" pointing to the tall cowboy. "He fits the description of the guy I asked you about a long time ago. There hasn't been any mention of him in forever, but there he is."

Sam pulled over to the side of the street and parked. He started to get out when Lindsay stopped him. "No!

Just get the license plate and we'll track it. We don't know who he is or if he is dangerous."

They waited until he had driven by then started towards Lindsay's house. Pulling into the garage, Sam said, "Stay here and let me check things out."

Lindsay laughed and followed him into the house. That's when she noticed Sam had a gun and was holding it straight out. "Sam, if he got in and brought someone else with him, he wouldn't have left him here."

Lindsay checked the sliders while Sam checked the front door. Sam went upstairs while Lindsay went downstairs. The safe was intact and untouched.

"Looks like he didn't get in. Nothing is missing. Maybe he was scoping things out for another visit. Maybe in the dark. Let's not worry about it. I want to have that talk now. I've waited long enough."

"As long as you are okay. Quite the day for adventure for you, huh?"

"Yes, but some are good. Like you being here. I miss you every time you disappear."

"I know and that's what I want to talk to you about. I'm sorry about that. And I will promise you right now, I'm done doing that."

"Really?"

"Yes, and I need to tell you why I do it so that you understand and you understand that I'm done leaving you."

Lindsay listened intensely while Sam poured his heart out. He summed up everything that Lindsay had concluded. She was just glad that he realized it.

"I'm asking you to help me not withdraw from you

and if you find me doing it, give me a little nudge. Sometimes I don't realize I'm doing it. And to show you how committed I am to you I want you to know that I want to spend the rest of my life with you."

"What are you saying?"

"I am going to propose to you, but I want you to think about it before I do. If you say yes, I will know that you have thought about it and won't have doubts because of the past. And now that I've told you it's coming you will know that I also have thought it over before I asked. I love you, Lindsay."

K endall was walking on air after the talk with her boyfriend. They had gotten things out in the open. She was finally able to feel like she could really trust him. She hoped he realized how much she loved him. She didn't think she would ever be able to put it in words. Because it was the first time for her.

When Jack called with the next assignment, she was excited.

"This is certainly a new Kendall. I haven't heard you this chipper in a while. What's going on with you?"

Kendall suspected Jack knew but she didn't feel the need to go into detail. Some things about her life, she wanted private and with no interference. She didn't trust Jack not to be as happy about things as she was.

"I'm well-rested and ready to go. Where am I going? What are we doing?"

"You are headed to Philadelphia. We've had some issues there lately and I think the cowboy guy you saw in

Dallas, the one that followed you and Joe, has been sniffing around Philadelphia. I am hoping you may be able to draw him out. You are the only one who has seen him and we think there is a connection to you."

"What's in Philadelphia that he would be sniffing around?" She couldn't believe it. This was almost like being handed things on a silver platter. She knew Langston, Elle, PJ Enterprises and Jack all had connections to Philadelphia.

"Remember that client that I mentioned to you a while ago that was followed? He was followed again a few times over the past week. And someone has been sniffing around the airport we fly in and out of on occasion."

Kendall hadn't been back to Philadelphia in forever so it wasn't her that Jack was referring to. If someone else was doing the same thing as she was, could this mean someone else was after the same information about Jack and the boss? Why was she the only one that had any incidents? Was it she he was after?

"Why Philadelphia? Doesn't sound like there is much there. Are we sure it's the same guy I saw?"

"We think so. Although no one has seen him except you, we have picked him up on street cams from the Philadelphia PD near one of our clients' offices. We think he let you see him. When you saw him in Dallas at the airport, he was in plain sight, not once but twice. He was in no hurry to hide from you. We think he wanted you to see him."

"I can't think of any reason why he would or any connection that we may have."

"Us either."

"I still don't understand why Philadelphia. I saw him in Dallas and ...." Kendall let that drop. She hadn't told Jack about the other times.

"And what?"

"And I have no connection to Philadelphia. I haven't done any jobs there."

"It's the only place we've found him. He was only in Dallas a day that we know of and he's been in Philadelphia a few different days."

"Have you picked him up on commercial flights?"

"No. We think he flies private charter but haven't been able to locate anything. It would help if we had a name too, which we don't. His facial recognition hasn't been useful due to the big cowboy hat he wears. It does well to cover his face."

"So, you actually haven't seen his face. You've seen a tall, brown-haired guy wearing a cowboy hat and boots near certain areas? That's pretty thin Jack."

"It seems so. But he's turned up too many times to ignore. The sooner we figure out what he is doing, the better. Any vehicle that he has used has come back with stolen plates or switched plates. Tracking those has sent us in circles and nothing solid. The guy is a professional, Kendall. We need to find out what he wants, what he is looking for and the connection to you. You won't ever be alone on this one. You will be protected at all times. We know you can take care of yourself, but we don't know how dangerous this guy is."

"That's comforting Jack. Like summoning a demon, just not knowing how evil it is."

"You leave Friday night, Kendall. Be ready."

Kendall had plans for Friday night. Now she had new plans and although Philadelphia was a silver platter, she still preferred her other plans over this. Yes, she had to admit it, she was in love.

43

B ecause the timing was off, Lindsay wasn't able to see Sam for a few weeks. Their conversations were on the telephone and Lindsay didn't like it.

"How have things been with the boys and Brad?"

"Still no contact. I actually broke down and called Brad. It was our first conversation without attorneys in years. I told him as a parent it was up to him to fix this and make amends. He didn't agree. Told me to mind my own business. He still doesn't think that the boys are my business, even after getting sole custody. I see another court date in my near future. He'll blame me for this too. He's amazingly good at twisting reality. I've told you about his sister, Barbie? She was there when I spoke to Brad so that didn't help much either."

"I'm sorry you have to deal with that. It's not right. He's lucky he has contact with the kids at all. Some of us aren't so lucky."

"Maybe it's time we fix that with yours."

"Lindsay, I appreciate your wanting to do that but

it's complicated with mine. It's best left alone until they are grown and out of her house. It's only a few more years."

"I'm sorry it's like that for you. Someday they will know how much you truly love them."

"I hope so Linds. I hope so. How is work going? Any more crazies?"

"There's always crazies in my environment. They keep life exciting."

"That they do. I miss you so much."

"I miss you too."

"Hey Sam, hold on." Lindsay had heard something. She set the phone down and went for her gun on the top shelf of the bookcase in the hallway on her way to the back door. She wasn't sure if what she heard was outside or inside. It sounded muffled so she couldn't be sure. Just as she came around the corner from the hallway into the dining room, someone ran out of the dining room into the kitchen and out the back door. He was tall but with no lights on and the darkness, that was all she could tell. She broke into a faster pace and moved toward the back door. She peered out the door, but couldn't see anything. As she switched the light on, she moved behind the kitchen wall for protection. She couldn't see anything or anyone. He didn't move that fast. She poked her head out the door in time to see him slip around the side of the house.

She bolted for the front door and yanked it open hoping to see him better if he was headed for the street and a car. Nothing.

She rarely turned the alarm on even when she was

home. She would have to be more vigilant in setting it. The boys were upstairs asleep and after securing the doors, she ran up to check on them. They were sound asleep and didn't know anything had happened. Typical Lindsay, calm as a cucumber, went back to the phone.

"Ok, I'm so sorry. I'm back."

"Is everything ok? What's wrong?"

"Oh, it was my neighbor at the door."

"At this hour? What did she want?"

"Drugs."

"What? Like Ibuprofen? You so have a way with words Linds."

Lindsay wasn't ready to tell Sam what had just happened. She needed to process it and she didn't need him lecturing her about the alarm system and its purpose. She was pretty sure it was the same tall guy that she had seen coming from the side of her house that time she and Sam had just returned home after getting back together. Why break in while she was home? Unless he had been in the house the whole time she was home. What was he after?

44

"Kendall, you will be flying into a private airport. It's the one that we have someone snooping around. Then you will be taken to an office to see if you are followed or if anything suspicious is around. You will have an escort the whole time."

"Jack, I don't like to question you but don't you think I'm more approachable if I'm alone?"

"Maybe Kendall, but I already warned you that you won't be alone. We know nothing about this guy and until we have something, that is how it has to be."

"Have you considered having one of ours follow me?"

"Yes, it was nixed."

"By whom?"

"Good luck, Kendall. I hope you get something. Anything, except hurt."

Kendall caught the flight on the private jet with Don, one of their own. With his square jaw and razor-sharp eyes, he was a stern-looking guy. When he smiled though, he could light up a room. Kendall always liked Don. He was built extremely well and quick as lightning. Jack sent one of their best to escort her.

It was a short flight and the pilot announced the runway in sight. Don moved to the cockpit with binoculars in hand. As he moved, he said, "Kendall, there is another pair on the table in the back. I'll focus on the airport and immediately surrounding it. Can you focus on the road out and buildings and parking lots around there, please?"

"On it." Kendall didn't like being told what to do but was glad Don took control this one time since her mind was on the last time she was here. This truly was a silver platter. She could see everything from Jack's view.

Just before touchdown Don came back and jumped in his seat, preparing for landing. "Kendall, he's there. Leaning against the building. We will walk in without much attention to him except a nod if he is still outside. If he is inside, same thing. We'll wait in the parking lot for him to leave, then we'll follow him. I have two other guys at the end of the street who will pick him up. Did you see anything?"

"Nothing suspicious, except your two guys who I already spotted. Black Camry. Glen and Scott." She wondered if it was the same Camry Jack used. She would know when she saw the license plate since she remembered everything. She hadn't taken the time to look through the binoculars since she would be close enough to check the license plate soon.

As they got off the airplane and headed towards the building, there was no one around.

They walked inside and saw their guy leaving out the front door. It was like he wanted to be seen. He could have been long gone.

They followed him out the door but by the time they got to the parking lot, there was no one there and only seven other cars that were all unoccupied. The cowboy had disappeared. He couldn't have gotten far or had to be on foot. She was tempted to suggest they look around the airport. She knew it wasn't very big with only four hangers and she also knew where everything was, although she would never admit that to Don. She liked him well enough and knew he had her back but didn't trust him with her personal mission. They could check security cameras later if he didn't follow them out.

They got in the Mercedes, Jack's Mercedes, and drove off. Don stuck to the speed limit and wasn't in a hurry to lose the cowboy should he want to follow them.

A minute after they passed the black Camry, Jack's according to the license plate, her phone dinged. She looked at the text. "It's Scott. Cowboy is following."

"Call Scott. Tell him we aren't going to the office. We'll go to the house. We can trap him in the neighborhood."

As they turned into the same neighborhood she had followed Jack into on Ainslie Street, she couldn't believe that they would go to the same house. This was definitely a silver platter. Don broke through her thoughts with, "He didn't turn. Glen and Scott will still follow him."

"Let me out right here. I am going for a jog. I'll meet you back here in a few."

"Kendall, no. We have explicit directions from Jack you are not to be alone at all."

Before he could object, Kendall jumped out of the car and started jogging through the backyards of the closest houses. Luckily, they were only driving about ten miles an hour. They weren't far from the convenience store she had parked in. As she made the short jog, she saw Cowboy sitting in the parking lot and Glen and Scott just pulling in. How could she get to him without them seeing her?

Before she could decide, Scott started walking towards Cowboy. Cowboy saw him and pulled out of the parking lot, turning in the opposite direction of the neighborhood. He made them.

She jogged back to where Don was waiting. He was furious. "No time for that! Turn around and make a left out of here."

"Kendall, I could kill you right now! What was that?"

"It was me trying to get to him before we lost him. I could have if Glen and Scott hadn't pulled in. We both know he wasn't going far after he didn't turn in this neighborhood to follow us."

"You have lost your mind. We still don't know anything about this guy or how dangerous he is."

"If he wanted to hurt me, he would have already. And you sound like Jack. How long have you worked with him now?"

"Long enough to know he will be furious when he finds out."

"Don't tell him, Don."

"Only if you promise not to go rogue again."

"Okay, can you get to the office we are going to from this direction?" Kendall didn't take time to argue with Don. It would have wasted time.

"Yes, call Glenn and Scott and let them know we are going to be passing by."

"What is going on that you and Jack know that I don't? Why am I not allowed to be alone on this trip?"

"You know as much as I do. Instructions from Jack. The same ones you got."

"I think there is more going on then you all are letting on. Wait, you guys think this guy is trying to get to me?"

"You are the only one who has seen him, until today. And I haven't seen his face, even through the binoculars, thanks to that stupid hat."

"But wait. You saw him today and the clients saw him when he followed them. I wasn't there for that and don't even know who the clients are. I think you guys are speculating a whole lot."

Kendall still wasn't willing to tell Jack or Don about the other times she had seen him. She didn't think he was after her, but something else. She would have to find out who the clients that he followed were but she knew Don wouldn't tell her. "By the way, where's Joe? He always drives."

"We didn't want him scaring off Cowboy at the airport. He's waiting for us."

The rest of the weekend passed by quickly. They did stay at a house on Langston Drive next to the house with the dog that Jack had gone into the last time Kendall was in Philadelphia.

She couldn't get close to Jack's house. The window blinds were all closed and she knew that house, like this one next door, had security alarms. There was no movement and no Jack all weekend. This made Kendall more suspicious and more curious. She would figure it out.

They did go to the office Jack had mentioned. It was in the same office building as she had found during her last trip where Elle, Inc. was but they didn't go to that office. They had gone to one on the third floor. It had "Private Investigators" on the door but wasn't listed on the directory. That is why she hadn't found this office last time she was here. How many offices did they need? She had tried to get back down to the Elle, Inc. office on the first floor but with the guys not leaving her side, she wasn't able to. She would have to come back again.

She had tried to persuade the guys to let her go for a walk and see if she could draw the cowboy out. He wasn't going to make a move with her having bodyguards everywhere she went. They insisted that was not going to happen until they had some information on the guy.

Kendall was awake at 2:30 a.m. She threw on some sweat pants and headed down the stairs for more water. Just as she approached the last step, Joe came in the front door. He tried to open it quietly, like he was sneaking back in. Kendall just looked at him and raised her eyebrow, in silent question. Joe raised his back. "I'm going for water, Joe, not running away.

She headed to the kitchen and as she was reaching for a glass, something just beyond the backyard caught her attention. A person was standing on the edge of the woods. Although they were a shadow in the light of the moon and she couldn't make out their face, she could tell it was a woman. "Joe, who were you talking to and why are they watching the back of the house?"

"Kendall! Duck! Joe was lightening quick in getting out the sliding glass doors that led to the backyard. He moved so fast; Kendall barely saw him. The shadow girl had moved the minute Kendall spotted her.

45

When Lindsay and Sam got together again after their long talk, there would be no proposing. Lindsay had the boys.

They took the boys to the mountains skiing. Lindsay loved to ski and hadn't done nearly enough of it. The boys, like her, were naturals.

They had a blast racing each other and the things they would bet on with each other was sure to be a future fight. Sam suggested that they had a bet on getting some of the prior winnings back from each other. He was a natural with the boys.

"Sam, you are awesome with them. Thank you for spending time with all of us. They adore you."

"Do they adore me as much as their Mom?" There was that grin. He still had it after all this time. "I used to do the same things with Tim when we were growing up. He would always bet me my favorite things and he usually won. Then later, after I would give them up to him, I would go steal them back."

"Did he know you stole them back?"

"Yes. The next time we would bet, he would want to bet on the things I stole back. I never could beat him so it was the only way. He only did it to prove he was better at everything than I was. He didn't really want my stuff."

"That's actually kind of funny. Are you two still betting on things?"

"Yeah and he gets frustrated because most of the time, I win now. Guess baby cousin grew up."

"That's cool that you were raised together. I guess it explains why you are so close and more like brothers."

"There isn't anything that I wouldn't do for him. He's been my lifesaver a few times and always there for me. Same for me with him. He had one thing I didn't think he would ever come back from. But he has for the most part."

"I'm sorry to hear that. He's pretty special. I really like Tim."

"Good because he is going to be my best man at our wedding, assuming you are going to accept when I ask." There was that beautiful grin. Lindsay didn't think she would ever get tired of it.

He had the ability to make perfect sense out of everything for her. Sometimes she would get on a rant and he would sit there and listen until she got it all out. He would look at her, grin and say, "Feel better now?" She always did. He was a great listener. And that grin could make her feel better even if she thought her world was falling apart. It was forever engraved in her memory.

Sitting in Jack's office across town from her house, Kendall was exhausted. She was also disappointed. Disappointed that there were no signs of the cowboy but more disappointed that she had been in Philadelphia and had no time to check out a few things. The guys stuck to her like glue when they left the house. She was lucky to go to the ladies' room without one of them guarding the door.

"Jack, that was a waste of time. I'm one of your best trained and there is no reason why the guys should have to play bodyguards. Had I gone out alone with them following me, we would have stood a better chance of seeing him or having him approach me."

"You may be right. Kendall, if we had something, anything, about who this guy is, it would be easier. He's like a ghost. I'm wondering if he doesn't want us to know he is around. He has made appearances enough for us to notice, yet no contact, no facial recognition because of that damn cowboy hat. We do know he is a professional. We know he moves around easily. We know he wants something, but what?"

"Jack, do you think you are giving him too much credit? I saw him in Dallas. Maybe it wasn't him. Cowboy hats and boots are the norms there. Maybe it was a look-alike. How would he know I was going to Dallas? We know he isn't one of us, well, you and the boss would know. But does he have a connection to one of us? What about Tall One? Maybe they are related. Is he still around by the way?"

"No. He is off the grid. But as soon as I find him, he'll be the first one questioned."

"It's not him. He may know something, though. They are both really tall."

"You sound pretty sure."

Kendall still hadn't told Jack she had seen him a few other times. "I saw his face in Dallas. Don saw him through the binoculars, not his face of course, in Philadelphia at the airport. Some of the other guys have seen him but not up close. The only thing they have in common is their height. What's the next move?"

"I hate to say it, but we wait. I just hope we figure him out quickly. He seems to have you figured out."

"Jack, is there anything that I should know? Is he trying to tell me something? Although I don't think I'm his target, you do."

"Nope."

Kendall didn't believe him for one minute. Jack had never lied to her before, but Kendall was convinced more than ever that he was hiding something. But what?

"Okay, now about the woman Joe chased? Who is she and what does she want?"

Jack knew this question was coming and he didn't want to tell her. There would be too much explaining needed and Jack wasn't up for it. None of it. Kendall already wanted to know things that Jack would kill for her not to know and this wouldn't help his stance. "We told you, she was a neighbor walking her dog." Jack was lying and Kendall knew it.

"Okay, Jack. Explain two things, she had no dog and she wasn't walking. Next time you want to lie, please give it a little more thought. Had you said she was looking for her run-a-way dog or cat in the woods, I may have believed you. Joe also knew her or he would not have hollered "duck. You know I hate liars!" Kendall had to walk out before she did something she would regret.

Jack let her walk out. He couldn't and wouldn't explain anything. He knew she hated liars. Most of what he did was to protect her. If Jack was going to be honest with himself, things were getting too deep.

47

It started out a typical day. Lindsay had gotten up, read the paper while drinking three cups of coffee and had showered. She was doing her hair when the phone rang.

Surprised to see that she had four missed calls, she answered.

"Hi, Mom. What's up?" Lindsay had only talked with her mother a few times a year and it was usually only when her mother needed something from her.

"Where have you been? Everyone is trying to get in touch with you."

"I was in the shower. What's going on? Oh, wait, Tim was one of the calls. This can't be good. I'll call you back."

Lindsay knew it had to do with Sam. Tim had never called her before. She called him back with sickness in her gut and shaking hands.

Before she could say anything, Tim said, "Lindsay, this is the worst call I have ever had to make in my life.

I'm not sure how to tell you this, but Sam is dead. Sam is dead."

Lindsay couldn't respond back. She couldn't breathe. She couldn't move. She couldn't blink. Her world just went black. She had a flashback to the morning of waking up to banging and a man in uniform with the Smokey the Bear hat standing in her living room. The morning she found out her father had died.

"Lindsay?"

"This is a sick joke. Who thought of this?"

"Lindsay, I'm sorry but it's true. I can't talk anymore right now but I will be in touch."

With that, Tim hung up. Lindsay stared at herself in the mirror and watched the tears fall silently down her face. Her soul registered it before her brain.

How? When? Where? What? Why? Why? Why? No, this was a mistake. The phone rang again. It was Ariel, the one mutual friend she and Sam had. Lindsay couldn't answer. She couldn't move. She couldn't breathe. Lindsay stood like that for what seemed like an hour. The phone rang several more times.

It took a minute for Lindsay to realize her doorbell was ringing. Sam! It had to be Sam! She ran for it.

Swinging the door open, Lindsay froze at the sight of Ariel. Lindsay couldn't talk. She moved aside to let her in.

Ariel took four steps in and stopped. She just stood there, waiting for Lindsay to say something. After several minutes, Ariel couldn't take Lindsay's silence.

"Lindsay, it's true. I'm sorry, but it's true. I don't have details…."

Ariel jumped when Lindsay threw the phone that she was still holding in her hand across the room and it busted, pieces flying everywhere. Lindsay walked over to the wall and laid her forehead on it. She still hadn't said a word. Ariel stood frozen. After what felt like an eternity, Lindsay turned around and slid down the wall to the floor. It seemed like slow motion. Her face was as white as a ghost and soaking wet from the silent tears that wouldn't stop. Ariel walked over and sat down beside Lindsay. They sat like that for what seemed like hours.

"How?"

"Gunshot. There were three people in the room. One was my nephew by marriage and the other was his uncle from the other side of the family. They were drinking liquor."

Lindsay jumped to her feet. "Now I know it's not true! Sam never drank liquor. He knew it made him stupid. It's all a lie!"

"Lindsay, I'm sorry, it's true. They were celebrating. Is there anyone else I can call for you?"

Lindsay moved as if on autopilot. She went to her office and came back a minute later. "Celebrating what? Can I use your phone?"

Ariel handed Lindsay her phone and watched her put a phone number in, text a message, then delete the message and the number. The text message Lindsay sent said, "Personal emergency. I'm fine. Don't come."

"Ariel, I need to be alone."

Lindsay had the same sickening, gut-wrenching feeling that she did the morning she found out her

211

favorite person in the world, her hero, her dad, was dead. It was the same one she had when she found out the truth about her dad from Harold. Was the story of her life that every man she loved would die and leave her? It wasn't fair that the only two people she loved in her life were both taken way to soon. Sadly, she had the same feeling that there was more to this story, too.

48

K endall had spent the past two weeks going through the motions. Jack called the third week and demanded to see her. He said if she wasn't coming to him at the office he would show up on her doorstep. She didn't want either but it was safer to go to him.

As Kendall breezed through the door, and before Jack could say anything she said, "I am not going to talk about it. I only have one question to ask you and if you ever thought about lying, now is not the time to do that. Did you have anything to do with it?"

"Kendall, first I'm sor...."

"Jack, just answer the question."

"No, Kendall. We are all deeply sorry."

"Fine, let's move on." Before Kendall could say anything more, Jack hugged her. It was the first time he had ever done that and it was a grip hug like he wanted to make sure she was still strong and not going to fall apart.

Although Kendall wanted nothing more than to fall apart right then, she couldn't. She wouldn't let Jack see her that way. She fell apart daily but not in front of anyone. Some days she couldn't breathe. Some days she wondered how she would carry on.

Releasing her and putting space between the two of them, Jack said, "Kendall, we have to talk about some of it. I need to make sure you are ready to go back to work and we are genuinely concerned."

"Jack, I need to work. I need to keep moving. I need to feel like I have a purpose." She also wanted to make sure that Jack hadn't had anything to do with it. She wasn't completely convinced. The details were sketchy and didn't make sense. She didn't know who to trust with anything anymore.

"Kendall if you think there are suspicious circumstances, let us look into it. It's the least we could do for you."

"No."

"You don't think this is job-related. I mean, to your job?"

"No."

"You haven't seen Cowboy again, have you?"

"No."

"Okay, Kendall, that is three one-word answers in a row. You are not fine. You are not ready. You are not well."

"Yes."

"Yes? Are you agreeing with me?"

"No! I am ready Jack. I have to be. We have work to

do." Kendall was more determined than ever to figure things out with her boyfriend, Jack, the boss, and the companies. Playtime was over.

49

Lindsay took the next two weeks off from the bar. She asked the owner to tell everyone she was visiting a sick relative out west. Only a few at the bar knew she was dating Sam. Lindsay didn't remember much about the last two weeks except going through the motions. She barely remembered the service.

Lindsay attended the service with Ariel. She had talked with his family members, whom she had only met a few times. She remembered looking at the pictures of him but had to walk away. It was too painful and lots of them were ones she had taken. Sam had a few years of pictures missing since he went through that rough period after his divorce. When they asked if anyone wanted to come up and talk about Sam, several eyes fell on her. She couldn't do it. She would never make it through. She didn't know how she was making it through standing here.

She remembered someone telling her that Sam had been cremated. She wanted to see his beautiful face one more time. It wasn't until after the service when she got almost out of the room, that it dawned on her that his urn was between the two 8X10 pictures of him. One was a baby picture that she had never seen and the other was one she had taken. She stopped dead in her tracks and looked back, then bolted from the room.

Several times a day she would have a breakdown or she would fall into a daze, then try to wake herself up from the nightmare. She cried continuously but somehow managed to pull herself together in front of the boys. They were devasted as well and old enough to understand. Sometimes when she was alone at night, she would whisper his name. It always brought tears. This was so unfair. She had already experienced this heartbreak once in her life, although it was a different love. She knew this insanely intense, extraordinary, fierce love for Sam was rare and that she would never have this again. Nor did she have a father's love. She didn't think she was unlovable, because they had both loved her immensely. Maybe she was cursed.

It was strange going back to work after two weeks off. Customers were asking how the sick relative was and she would just say much better. She was a little uncomfortable with the lie but would feel much worse if she had to deal with questions about the death of her boyfriend that most didn't know she had. Lindsay of all people hated lies, but this one didn't affect anyone.

Lindsay couldn't say his name without losing her breath. How could she live without him?

50

Most days, Jack kept Kendall on a tight leash and always surrounded by others on short in and out jobs. They tiptoed around her. She couldn't take it anymore so she told them to knock it off. She wasn't going to break down on them. She was good.

About six months after Kendall had returned to work, she was on a job in San Diego. She loved the charming, clean city. It was much smaller than she had thought it would be and easy to move around. She loved going to new places and sightseeing around the courthouses when time permitted. Since her boyfriend's death, she was taking life a little slower and trying to enjoy things more. She had always had a fascination with courthouses. San Diego had just built a new one and she wanted to see it.

This particular job was getting into a warehouse to review manifest on shipping containers. She had gone in with one of the government organizations that occasionally hired her, through Jack. Always through Jack.

Scott Preston, a talented FBI agent, was sent in with her. She had worked with Scott a few times over the years. This was a job she could have done on her own since it was getting into the office at night with light security. It was easy to mess with the camera feeds as long as Kendall was inside. One would think the warehouses along the docks would have tighter security but with as much as they were checked on by state and federal agencies, it wasn't worth it. And most weren't doing illegal things.

This particular owner was being blackmailed into accepting some illegal containers. The blackmailer was watching the owner, but not so much their shipment unless they had a guy on the inside and Kendall would be avoiding any contact. The owner was leaving some information in the office but it was too much to carry out and faster for Kendall to read through it with her memory. They also suspected there were clues left for the end receiver of the containers, in some of the documents.

Once inside, Scott looked at Kendall and said, "Hey, I'm sorry about your boyfriend. We were all devasted for you. We heard it was pretty serious between the two of you."

"Wow, news travels fast, huh? Thank you. I appreciate that, Scott"

"You know, Kendall, in this business, having friends and people you can trust is rare. I just want you to know I'm one of those rare friends for you."

"Thanks, Scott. I appreciate that, too. Where are you based out of these days?"

"Philadelphia. Been there for about two years."

Kendall wasn't sure if she should be excited or suspicious. "What are you doing on this case in San Diego? A little far from home."

"I was here for four years prior to transferring to Philadelphia. I was one of the lead agents on the blackmailer's cases those few years. This isn't his first time. Sadly, I was never able to put him away. He's a slippery guy and leader of a large organization. That's why we are handling this one a little differently and why we brought you in on it. Less movement from us is better and with your photographic memory. Well, you know.

"I see. How do you like Philadelphia?"

"It's good. I prefer the weather here but like that area better. I needed fresh eyes and they needed the same. It's working."

They spent the next few hours going over documents and catching up. "Ding, ding, ding! We have a message!" Scott pulled out his Canon camera and Kendall showed him the documents to photograph. The rest she would write a report on for them."

"No wonder you have the reputation you do, Miss Kendall. Well done. We weren't expecting you to find the message. You just saved us some serious man-hours and time. Are you sure you don't want to work for us?"

"Are you in town at least the rest of the day? I have time to check out the courthouse before I fly out. I'll hear you out." Kendall had no interest in changing jobs or companies. She didn't think Jack would let her go easily anyway. She had an interest in seeing if she could trust him and she was planning on seeing the courthouse anyway.

"Sure, I would love to. Let's get out of here if you are ready and we can check-in at the office, then head over. It's close enough to walk and by then, it will be open. Coffee time."

Lindsay was just walking in the door of her house from dropping the boys off at summer camp when her phone rang. She hated "unknown caller" and rarely answered. But since Sam's death six months ago, she had been answering them. Not right now. She was tired.

As she set her things down, the phone rang again. "Unknown caller." She clicked answer but didn't say anything. She could hear an odd noise but couldn't make it out. It was the same as the four other calls she had answered in the past two months. She would listen for about two minutes hoping whoever it was would say something or she would figure out the noise. It would quickly irritate her so she was always the first to hang up.

As she started for the kitchen, the phone rang again. Without looking at who it was she picked it up and screamed, "Either say something or stop calling me!"

"Lindsay? It's Tim."

"Tim? I am so sorry. I thought you were someone else."

"Apparently. Just for the record, this is the first time I've called you. I have to apologize for that. It's been uhhhh, rather hard. I'm sorry Lindsay."

"No apology necessary. I can't imagine how you feel."

"Thanks. You either. I was wondering if we could get together and talk?"

"Of course. When is it convenient for you?" Lindsay hadn't spoken to Tim since the day of Sam's funeral. She had wanted to contact him but wasn't sure what to say to him. She wanted some answers so she waited him out, knowing he would eventually contact her.

"Right now. I'm about ten minutes away if it works for you."

"Yes, I would like that. See you in a minute."

Ten minutes later, with nerves on edge Lindsay opened the door for Tim.

They just looked at each other for a moment, neither one knowing what to say. Lindsay moved aside so Tim could come in. As Lindsay turned around from closing the door, Tim swooped her up into a bear hug. When they pulled apart about five minutes later, both had tears streaming down their faces.

"Be right back." Lindsay went and grabbed a box of tissues. She had them in almost every room these days. She tried pulling herself together.

"Here you go. I'm glad you called, Tim. How are you?"

"I won't lie. It's been tough. He was not only my

cousin but more like my brother and my best friend. A huge part of me is gone."

Lindsay wasn't sure what to say, "You know he loved you like a brother and best friend also. He thought the world of you."

"Yeah, I know. I just wish I could have done something. Anything. Lindsay, I know you want more information. I know it's hard to digest. I'm still expecting him to call or walk in the door. I'm sure you feel it too. I'll tell you what I can but there really isn't much to tell."

"Tim you aren't responsible and Sam would never want you to carry that burden. He was a grown man and made a bad decision. Although, I still don't understand."

"Yeah, they were celebrating the one guy's release from prison after twenty years. They weren't even friends. He was his friend's uncle. I'm not sure who brought out the liquor, but it was Sam's gun. They ruled it accidental suicide, Lindsay. I'm not sure if they were just looking at it or playing around. I'm sure Sam didn't realize there was a bullet in it. But then again, I'm blaming the liquor. I should have checked on them." With that, Tim broke down and sobbed heavily.

Lindsay put her arms around him and hugged him tight while he cried it out. "Tim, you can't do this to yourself. You know Sam would be devastated if he knew you were thinking you are responsible. It's not yours to claim."

Once Tim pulled himself back together a little, he said, "Thank you, Lindsay, you're right. That is the last thing he would want. I haven't been able to tell anyone else this and it's a relief to get it out and have you remind me Sam would be devasted and furious. I'm sorry, I came here to give you answers to what little I know and console you and look at me."

"Tim, it's okay. I know how hard this is for you. I get it. Sadly. I don't think I will ever get past this. Are you sure it was accidental suicide? It's still not sitting right with me. Maybe because it didn't have to happen this way."

"Lindsay, I'm sure they did powder residue testing of all three to confirm who fired. The other two guys that were there are both devastated."

"How much do you know about the uncle who just got out of prison?"

"Not much. I've talked to Ariel. She doesn't know much about him either. I'm assuming the police checked him out pretty closely. They would have brought charges against him if he had any responsibility in it."

"I will never understand."

Lindsay and Tim talked for a few more hours about Sam and how much he meant to both of them. Not much else was said around the circumstances of his death. Lindsay brought out pictures, and they reminisced.

"I wanted to ask you if you would mind making some copies of the photos. You know we, the family, don't have many. He wouldn't really take pictures until you."

"Absolutely. I'll drop them off to you next week."

"Thanks, Lindsay. You are the best. We know why Sam loved you so much. Oh, I was asked to give you this." He handed her a piece of paper that looked like it had been ripped off a hotel notepad.

The only thing that was written on the paper was a telephone number. "Who gave it to you? Whose number is it?"

"I don't know who the guy was. He was tall with brown hair and wore cowboy boots and a hat. Just asked me to give you this number with the message that if you are ever in trouble, you can call that number. I thought it was a little strange but he walked off and didn't stop when I started asking questions. I figured you knew him. But if you did, you would have had his number."

"When did he give this to you?"

"At Sam's funeral. I'm sorry Lindsay. I kind of forgot about it with all my grief and being in a fog. I found it in my wallet today and that was another reason I finally called you."

Lindsay just looked at the paper with the handwriting but didn't recognize it. Tim got up to leave and slowly they walked to the front door. They hugged for a long time and promised to keep in contact.

As soon as the door closed, Lindsay leaned against it with her back and slid to the floor in slow motion. The tears fell like a floodgate that had been long closed and busted open.

Sometime later, the tears stopped and her vision finally cleared. She still couldn't move and as she sat there with so many unanswered questions, she caught sight of a box on the end table where Tim had been sitting.

She slowly made her way over to it. She stared at it

for a long time, not sure if she wanted to open it. When she finally couldn't take it anymore, she opened it and a piece of paper fell out.

"Lindsay, I know Sam would want you to have this. I didn't hand it to you personally because, well, I'm not sure I could watch you open it. He couldn't wait to give this to you and make you his wife forever. He loved you more than life itself Lindsay. You made him a better person." Lindsay noticed the little crinkles where Tim's tears had fallen. She added her own to it as she stared at the beautiful engagement ring and thought about all their plans that would never be. She needed a drink. She rarely drank but this called for a little sip of vodka. Or two.

Settling down with her drink, she picked up the paper with the phone number on it.

5 2

Kendall and Scott walked out onto the sidewalk and headed towards the new courthouse in San Diego she wanted to see.

"It's really good to see you again, Kendall. Thanks for inviting me along."

"Scott, it's always good to see you. You truly are one of my favorites. But don't tell the others. They'll be jealous so let it be our secret."

"I love a good secret."

That was interesting for him to say. Kendall was wondering if she could trust him with secrets and how trustworthy he truly is. She would put him to a test. It would take time and she had plenty of that lately.

"What's your best-kept secret?"

"Now if I told you that, it wouldn't be my best kept anymore."

This was a good start. "Okay, you tell me one and I'll tell you one of mine."

"Then they wouldn't be secrets. Really, how are you

doing Kendall? I know you have that steel exterior but really, how are you?"

"Did Jack put you up to this questioning? That sounds like something he would say."

"No. You know you have quite a reputation, Kendall. You are known for very few things and most don't know much about you. None of us knew you had a boyfriend or anything about your personal life and wouldn't have if not for…. well, the tragedy of it. You are known for being precise, fearless and that steel exterior. You are really the best of the best."

"Are you trying to flatter me into working with the bureau?"

"Nah, that wouldn't work with you."

"Well, thank you for the flattery then. I appreciate it." She gave him a sincere smile. One of her first in a very long time. Something, or someone, wiped it clean off her face as she looked over towards the courthouse.

Scott noticed immediately and followed her gaze. "Do you know him?"

Leaning up against the front of the building, off to the far-right side, was Cowboy.

Cowboy was looking at her with a straight face. No expression whatsoever.

"Would you mind staying here, Scott. I'll be right back." This said even as Kendall started to walk away towards Cowboy. It wasn't a question.

"Kendall."

"Stay there, Scott."

Kendall was already crossing the street caddy corner

to the beautiful courthouse towards the tall cowboy who hadn't moved or taken his gaze off Kendall.

As Kendall reached the other side of the street and started walking toward Cowboy, he easily moved away from the building and disappeared around the corner and out of Kendall's sight. Kendall picked up her pace to just short of a jog. Scott started across the street once he saw the cowboy had rounded the corner of the building and Kendall sped up her pace. He couldn't see him and wanted to stay close to Kendall.

As Kendall rounded the corner of the building and stopped, she caught sight of Cowboy a block away, crossing the street and disappearing into an alley. He didn't look back at her. Damn his long legs. Just as she started after him, Scott caught up to her. "Kendall, wait! I can't let you go after him alone."

Kendall continued her fast pace. She was furious. "Tell Jack you lost me."

"I can't do that. The instructions were specific."

Kendall didn't respond as she cursed Jack six ways internally. She kept up her fast stride, just short of a jog. Scott kept up, too. As they came to the spot where she had last seen Cowboy, they found an empty alley. Kendall broke out into a run, watching both sides of the alley for anything or anyone. Scott keeping pace with her.

As they reached the end of the alley, it opened back up onto a main street. Kendall and Scott stopped, both looking all around. He was gone. Vanished.

"Scott! If you had not followed me, he may have

spoken to me!" Kendall was so furious and frustrated she couldn't see straight.

They continued to stand there looking around for five minutes, without speaking. Kendall finally turned and headed up the sidewalk back to the front of the courthouse. She was too furious to say anything and Scott didn't know what to say. He promised Jack he would look after her until she flew out.

"Kendall, I'm sorry. Jack filled me in and asked me to watch out for you. I agree with Jack. Until you all know more, you shouldn't be alone."

"Scott, I don't have anything else to say to you other than I'm sorry. I like you and was starting to trust you. You aren't one of the rare ones. You are one of them."

"You make it sound like we are against you, Kendall."

"I will tell you what I told Jack. If I can get alone with him.... never mind. I'm beating a dead horse." Kendall was too mad to stop and take in the beautiful courthouse.

Lindsay stared at the piece of paper with the number for a long time. She was deeply saddened by Tim and him feeling responsible and his grief, and by not having any more answers than she previously had.

She didn't know what to make of this number. Cowboy had been in her house. He could have left that number then. He could have just talked to her instead of running off. What was he looking for? She still hadn't figured that out. She hadn't seen him at Sam's funeral. She should have asked Tim where exactly Cowboy had given him that paper.

Should she call it? He was specific it was only if she were in trouble. Was he looking out for her? Why? Why was he threatening people to stay away from her? It was all too much. She racked her brain to think of any reason that she would be in danger.

She had no enemies except Mark, Brad and Barbie. Maybe her mother and brother. Mark hadn't found her and she had never heard from him or anything about him since she left. Brad wasn't dangerous. He was angry, but Lindsay didn't think dangerous. He did promise to make her life a living hell. Brad would rather see her suffer slowly than kill her quickly. Barbie was crazy but if she were going to do something, it probably would have been years ago to get custody of the boys when the boys were younger. Then again, she was crazy. There were a few others in Lindsay's life that were disturbed but none that were crazy enough to come after her.

This guy was going through a lot of trouble just to try and freak her out. Maybe he was to take the focus off Brad and Barbie. She hadn't heard from Rob or any of the crazies in her past. The boys were getting older and could almost choose where they wanted to live. It wasn't with Brad but he would never realize that. It didn't make sense for him to offer a number to call if she were in trouble if he were the one putting her in danger of some kind.

Cowboy had never threatened Sam. If he were warning people to stay away from her, the most likely to be warned would have been Sam. None of it made any sense.

Should she call the number? How did he know if Tim remembered to give it to her? For all he knew, she didn't have it.

Lindsay picked up the box with the engagement ring and fell asleep clutching it.

5 4

Kendall stormed into Jack's office upon her return from San Diego. She was furious! "Jack! Where are you?"

No answer. She checked the bathroom and supply room off the main office. Empty. She started down the hallway to the back offices. She checked the first one on the left. Empty. She continued down to the end of the hallway to Jack's personal office. Empty. She headed back to the front. Empty. Jack never left the office open.

She went out the front door. She felt the hair on her neck and arms stand straight up and felt eyes on her as she walked out. She hadn't noticed anything amiss on her way in because she was so furious with Jack and focused on berating him. She stopped, standing perfectly still. No one was around and everything was still. There were lots of vehicles in the parking lot, but all appeared empty as she scanned over them. Jack's Mercedes was in its usual spot. Still standing perfectly still, Kendall moved only her eyes, as she took in the scenery.

Four guys were watching her from various windows on the top two floors of the building across the street. She recognized Joe, their driver. More of Jack's guys were visible. Two on the rooftops of each building next to the one directly across the street. One on the sixth floor of the next building watching her from the window. It was Cowboy.

Her phone vibrated in her hand. She looked at the text. "Walk to your car like normal. Get in it. And drive away like everything is ok. Now." It was from Jack. But where was he? Then a second message. "Move!"

For once, she did as he instructed. She drove five miles down the road before pulling into a coffee shop. Kendall could not go into a coffee shop and not order coffee.

This silence was eerie. She texted Jack back, "What is going on?" No answer.

A minute later, Jack walked into the coffee shop just as she sat down with coffee in hand. He was furious.

"Let's go." He turned around and walked to his car. Kendall had no choice but to follow.

As they got into the car, a black Camry, Kendall demanded to know what was going on. Jack didn't say anything until they reached a crowded parking lot where he pulled in. Kendall knew he was making sure they weren't followed.

"Jack. Talk to me."

"Kendall, I wish you hadn't shown up. We were so close. You know the office is for emergencies only, or if I need to know you are coming."

"What is going on. I want answers now. I know this has to do with Cowboy."

"Really? How would you know that?"

She wasn't going to tell him that she had seen him in one of the windows. "Because it seems everything concerning you, this job and my life are centered around this mysterious man in a cowboy hat."

"I should have kept you up to speed on the situation. Two nights ago, Cowboy went to the office, got in without setting off the alarm, and left me a note. It said he was watching." Jack wasn't hiding his feelings. He was furious.

"Watching? Watching what? Who?" Kendall hadn't told Jack yet that she had seen him in San Diego. But she knew Scott had. That is why she stormed into his office amidst this mess. Whatever it was.

"It didn't say anything more, just that he was watching. Since we still don't know who he is or what he wants, we don't have any idea. We only know one thing and that he's a professional."

"Professional what? Stalker? This is crazy." Kendall hadn't told Jack about all the other connections Cowboy had made with her. She still hadn't figured out his game either.

"Kendall, that's what is so infuriating. This has been going on for a long time. We can't catch him. He is as elusive as they come. I left a message for him last night at the office, on the door. He got it."

"Okay, so he came back? What did your note say? Why did he come back? Let me guess, still no face?"

"Yes, he came back and got the note. We have him

237

on camera. No face. That damn hat blocks it. I think he is rather enjoying this cat and mouse game. The note said for him to meet me at the office today and we could settle this. He left a note back, but inside again, saying he would return today."

"So that explains the guys watching from the buildings. It doesn't explain why you were not inside when I went in."

"I had gone out through the supply room. There's a door that leads to the office next door. I was waiting there with reinforcements. We wanted him to come in and catch him off guard first with the empty office."

"Well, so much for that, Jack. I don't see Cowboy walking into your office in the broad daylight. He's been way too careful and only been seen when he wants to."

"I still think this has to do with you, Kendall. You have seen him more than anyone else. Maybe I should ask you what you are doing to attract him."

"Except you, Jack. You may not have seen him but he's been around you more than me. Are you sure I'm not a pawn to get to you?" Kendall didn't believe that for a minute and neither would Jack if he knew everything. But he didn't.

"Could be but my gut is telling me it's you."

"Then the only other option is to let me pull him out. That will only happen if I'm alone. Scott blew it in San Diego. Or rather you did by recruiting Scott for your cause. That's why I was here today. How could you bring in an outsider? Why not send one of our guys?"

"You would have spotted them or you would have

resisted had I tried to send one. I wasn't up for the argument."

"Well, that didn't get you anywhere, Jack. And lost me the opportunity to have a face to face, up close and personal with Cowboy." Kendall's voice was strained, clearly indicating to Jack how furious she was.

As Jack pulled back up to Kendall's car at the coffee shop, he let out a low whistle, "I've got a meeting I have to get to. I'll be in touch with a new approach later today or tomorrow."

"Can I come? You are going to meet with the boss, aren't you?"

"Get out. And don't follow me. You will be wasting your time."

55

Lindsay slept on that phone number for more than one night. There was so much going on, she didn't know if she was ready for the outcome of making that call. She thought about having it traced but she knew it would come up empty. He was too smart for that. She was tired. Exhausted really. She suspected Cowboy would show himself again.

Lindsay threw herself into work. She didn't have much except work and the boys right now, but she was okay with that. She loved the boys and she loved this bartending gig. She had surprisingly stayed with it longer than she had intended.

She toyed with the idea of going back to work in the legal field. This was where she needed to be for now. It was easy, fun and not consuming. She had enough other things occupying her mind right now. She still missed Sam. She had picked the phone up a few times to call him, then remembered.

"Hey, Drama Llama! Good to see you. Where have

you been? You either have a girlfriend or been in jail. I doubt it was jail so do tell. Who is she?"

"You don't miss much do you?"

"Nope. I find when my customers disappear, it's one of the two reasons. Hopefully, not both."

"She's great! I really like this one. I met her through a mutual friend. I don't have the connection you did with…. you know." His face turned red and he was sorry he brought it up.

"You know you can say his name. Not like I forgot. I like talking to you about him. And I hope everyone finds someone like I did. I truly do. It's the best feeling in the world. And also, the most devastating when it ends."

"I hear ya'. It's kind of taught me not to take anything for granted."

"I'm glad you found a reason in it, because I sure haven't, but maybe one day. So how long has it been?"

"Just a few weeks."

"Yup, about the time you disappeared."

Lindsay walked off to wait on other customers when Ariel came in. Lindsay hadn't seen much of her. "Hey, you! How are you?"

"Hey, Linds. I mean Lindsay, sorry. I'm good. Look, I can't stay but can you grab me a soda, please?" Even Ariel knew on the rare occasions Sam used her name, he shortened it.

"Sure, are you okay?"

With an overly bright smile, "Yes, don't look concerned."

Lindsay had gone to get her soda and when she placed it on the bar, Ariel said with a smile, "Act like this conversation is a good one. Keep smiling. No frowning. Don't say anything, just listen."

"Okay, what is wrong with you?" Lindsay said it while smiling.

"I have a message for you. Don't ask me who it's from. I don't know. It was in my driver's seat when I got in my car. It just said to tell you that the bar and your house are bugged. There is a tracker on your car. They are watching you. Don't remove anything, just be aware."

With a smile, "What the hell are you talking about? Who is watching me?"

"I don't know. That was the message. It said to act friendly and casually. Are you in some kind of trouble, Lindsay?"

With a big smile, "No, everything is normal. My new normal. I have no idea what this is about. But I'll find out."

Ariel tapped both hands on the bar and pushed off her barstool. "See you later Lindsay. Take care."

"You too and no worries, I got your soda!" Ariel was almost out the door and just waved.

Lindsay wished Sam were here to talk to about this.

"She was certainly a chipper one!"

"Yes, Drama Llama, much like you today."

56

K endall didn't follow Jack, only because she had somewhere else to be. She suspected he was probably going to Philadelphia. It seemed most things she had discovered were based out of there. She would need to make time to get back and do more research. She had taken a break from her quest of finding out about Jack, the boss, and the companies. With everything going on, including her boyfriend's passing, which still didn't make sense, and her questions around that plus this Cowboy, and her suspicion that she was being watched by Jack, she didn't want to risk anything.

Kendall felt she was spinning in circles with each new thing she learned. Everything was a loop that didn't end and went nowhere. They had been in business well before she came along so they had plenty of time to cover their tracks.

That was it! Why cover their tracks? What did they have to hide? Yes, they did illegal work and usually did things the Feds wouldn't or couldn't do, but the Feds knew about them. Kendall had no doubt that the Feds, nor anyone else, knew most of what this organization really does, but they didn't need to because they were valuable to the Feds when they needed them.

The average American had no idea this organization existed and they didn't conduct regular investigations. Hence the need for covers, covert operations and extremely wealthy clients.

Kendall thought back on all the people she did know from the organization. It was only a handful. She couldn't really say if someone from a past job with the organization was involved. She knew that recruits for the organization were everywhere and all had a specific purpose. Some were just fill-ins, some were distractions, some were covers for the top ones like Tall One was for her although he did other things in the organization as well. Kendall hated the fact that she sometimes needed a cover guy to give her the appearance of having a "normal" life.

Tall One. Kendall did have to wonder if he were involved in any way with Cowboy. They were both professionals, both were very tall and both had a connection to her and excellent at disappearing. If Tall One was involved, he would have made an appearance of some kind by now. Unless Cowboy was doing it for him. Cowboy did seem to be watching her and keeping tabs on her. It was unsettling how he knew where she was going to be, like Dallas and San Diego. Did he have an inside connection? Kendall had considered he was hired by Jack to freak her out and maybe distract her from investigating him and the boss if he suspected she was. But after the last time she was at Jack's office to chew him out over San Diego, she didn't think he would go to that much trouble. But would he? He did go through extremes for her not to meet the boss.

Kendall couldn't decide if she should contact Tall One. He had worked for Jack and those that did were well tested and trained to an extreme, including psychological testing. Unless they were used as covers. Then they were involuntary participants, like the computer geek.

Kendall wasn't an involuntary participant. She was picked. Selected. Trained. Tested. All before she knew it. All before she understood it. How many others? So many questions, so few answers.

Kendall knew one answer. Cowboy is not part of the same organization as she. Who is he? Does he work for someone, other than Jack? The questions were endless.

She ultimately concluded she would not go to Tall One. He couldn't be trusted and had issues.

L indsay finished off her day and the boys were at their dad's house for the night. She settled down to relax with a cup of coffee and read a book to take her mind off everything. She was starting to burn out. She was on page four of the book before she realized she had no idea what she has just read. Her mind had wandered.

First, Tim giving her that number, with which she had done nothing, and now Ariel giving her this message about being bugged, tracked and watched. As she sat in her living room, she started looking around, moving her eyes, but not her head. Because she was reading, she had the overhead light on and two lamps. The room was lit up more than usual.

Lindsay looked first at the tv and all its surrounding gadgets. The cable box, the WIFI, modem, the surround sound. She wondered if there was a camera in any of those. There was nothing out of the ordinary. She regretted being a clean freak now and wished she had let dust pile up for once, then she may have seen traces of things moved or dust wiped off by fingerprints.

She moved her eyes over to the bookshelf. She didn't collect anything because she moved too much and hated packing knickknacks. There was a ceramic statue that she had made when she was a kid. She loved the two stone figurines she had picked up in Aruba, her first out of the country trip with one of the boyfriends. She also loved the elephants that were on the second shelf. They were given to her when her grandmother passed away. The photo albums were filled with pictures of the boys. There was nothing there to hide a camera or lens in or on.

Lindsay moved her eyes to the digital thermostat next to the bookshelf. There was nothing out of the ordinary. The only things left were the pictures on the wall. There was the beach picture she had given Brad on their first anniversary. When she left him, she had taken it with her since he never liked the beach anyway. She didn't see any holes in it and knew it would only have to be a pinhole. She picked her head up now and really looked at the picture. She got up, went into the kitchen and came back with Windex. It needed a good cleaning anyway. She lifted it off the wall gently and leaned it against the couch. Stepping back, she sprayed the Windex directly on the glass. As she gently wiped it off, she looked closely at every spot. Nothing noticeable. Once the glass was cleaned, she flipped it over and inspected the back. Nothing. She put it back on the wall. Lindsay took the other two pictures down and repeated the cleaning and inspecting. Nothing.

This was ridiculous. She was paranoid in her own house. Did he, whoever "he" was that left that paper in Ariel's car, just do this to freak her out? She was beginning to think it was Brad, or his sister, playing with her sanity. They had another court date coming up.

If it were Brad, she could only imagine what the "emergency number" was that he had given to Tim through the Cowboy. It was probably so he could get someone there if she were in trouble of some kind to witness her fall. As for Cowboy, he was probably to make her paranoid too. Good going, Brad and company. Lindsay was tempted to call the number just to see what happened. Not yet. Now that she thought she had it figured out she would wait them out.

5 8

K endall entered Jack's office happy and excited. "Hey, Jacko! Glad to see you are alive and well and no one has shot you."

"What is up with you and why would you say that?" Jack realized he would never figure Kendall out. He didn't understand how she could compartmentalize like no one he had ever known. Except for the boss. She wasn't moody but she could flip her mind like a light switch. When she was focused on something, she didn't give up until she figured it out. When she was ready to move on, she moved on. When she was done with something, she was done.

"I'm over all of this mystery and want to get back to doing my job. I'm over the drama and trying to figure things out. Whatever happens, I'll deal with then. If you want to keep trying to figure Cowboy out, have at it. I think we are overthinking this. Maybe if we ignore him, he will slip up. He probably won't like being dismissed."

"Kendall, what do you know that you aren't telling me?"

"Not a thing. I just don't think he is as significant as we have been giving him credit. Look, Jack, I don't have anything for him, no information, no missing people, nothing. I haven't done anything that I need to worry about having someone watch me for. If he thinks I have and I'm ignoring him, he will have to come out with it."

"I see."

"Now the question you have to ask yourself, Jack, is there anything you need to worry about like that? If not, good. If so, fix it so he goes away. Done. Let's move on."

"Kendall, I want to be you when I grow up. Everything is black and white with you, isn't it?" Jack knew Kendall made decisions quickly and effectively. She either rarely analyzed anything or she analyzed it so quickly and effectively, it appeared she didn't give it any thought. Did that make sense? He would think about it later.

"Okay, Jack work on that. What's next. I'm anxious to do something good, or bad. Whatever, just put me to work."

"Glad to hear you say that. You are off to Indianapolis."

"Great! I haven't seen that courthouse. Leave me time to explore. You can even have one of the guys go with me but I'm over that, too."

As convincing as Kendall was, Jack didn't think she was being honest with him about letting this all go.

As well as Jack knew Kendall, he still couldn't tell

when she was lying. She didn't do it often, but when she did, she was really that good. She had great influences.

SHE DID HER JOB IN INDIANAPOLIS WITHOUT INCIDENT. IT was a boring one getting into that CPA's office and finding the attic room filled with the second set of books he kept for his clients. She was only interested in the one client who was selling his casino in Las Vegas to a rival. It didn't make sense why he was selling to this client in particular and at a very fair price. She had found the books and found the records. He was losing money rapidly. That's what you get when you have a streak of bad luck and a new girlfriend you think you need to impress. Men. She would never understand them. It wasn't some devious plan like the buyers had suspected. No setup. Just stupidity.

She was headed off to explore the courthouse. She knew Jack had Joe following her and she had considered inviting him to walk with her and explore, but she preferred to do it alone. She usually parked a few blocks away. She liked the walk leading to courthouses since they were usually filled with coffee houses and cafés. She could always get a job as a coffee marketer if this one stopped working out.

Kendall was standing on the corner opposite the courthouse, taking it all in. The outside was beautiful but she couldn't wait to get inside. This courthouse had an intriguing history and at one time, the post office had been part of the courthouse.

Kendall entered the front of the building on the first

floor where the glass mosaic tiles on the ceiling were as impressive as they were magnificent. What was even more impressive and beautiful were the two self-supporting marble staircases. Kendall had to walk on them.

She walked up the staircase from the first floor to the second. At the top, she looked back to see Joe standing on the first floor looking at her. She ignored him and moved along the second floor towards one of the courtrooms. The court was not in session so she opened the door and went in. She was alone. If she wanted to stay that way, and possibly give Cowboy an opportunity to present himself, she would have to lose Joe.

She went to the front of the courtroom and to the door on the right. She knew of the two doors on either side of the Judge's bench that one opened to Judge's chambers and the other was where any prisoners were brought into the courtroom. From the location of this courtroom, she guessed she wanted the door on the right.

As she slipped out the door, she took one last glance back. No Joe. She found her way to the prisoner elevator and back to the first floor. As she walked out the nearby exit door, she found herself on the side of the building, closer to the back of the courthouse then where she entered through the front. She walked the opposite direction, going further away from the front entrance. Kendall knew Joe would be furious, but she decided she could live with that.

As she got to the end of the building, she turned back around to see Cowboy coming towards her and not far away. She was safe here but if Joe did figure out what she was doing, he would be close behind. She turned back around and started walking again. As she got to the corner, she saw a café on the opposite side of the street. She moved at a fast pace and went inside.

She waited. With his long legs, it didn't take Cowboy long to catch up to her. As he walked in, they instantly made eye contact. Neither one broke it until he was standing directly in front of her.

She checked the door and the front of the shop for Joe. "I am going to guess you have about 30 seconds."

"Not even. Don is coming too. Closer than Joe. I'm on your side. You may be in danger. Stop trying to figure things out. They know. I'll be in touch. Stay alert. Order coffee now." And just like that, he disappeared out the back.

As Kendall was standing in line, Don came rushing in and almost knocked a few people over. "Where is he?"

"Joe? He is probably right be…."

"I'm not talking about Joe and you know it," Don said this between his teeth. He was furious.

"I came in and went to the ladies' room to wash my hands then got in line. I haven't seen anyone here except you." Taking a step and turning to the barista, she ordered a large coffee.

As she was ordering Don went out the back and at the same time, Joe came in the front door. "Where are they?"

"Don just came in and asked where "he" was then

headed out the back as you came in the front. What am I missing?"

"Are you trying to say you didn't see Cowboy?"

"Did you?" Kendall almost looked surprised.

"What was that all about? Going out the side door? What were you thinking?"

"Joe, I'm not having this conversation with you right here, right now. And I wasn't trying to lose you if that is what you are referring to."

As Lindsay got her coffee and paid for it, Joe clicked his earpiece. Giving Lindsay a contemptuous look, he said, "Let's go."

Once out on the sidewalk, Don joined them. "Lost him. He's not a damn Cowboy, he is a ghost."

"He's a good one because for once I didn't see him. As I told Don when I went into the coffee shop, I walked straight into the ladies' room to wash my hands then as I came out and got in line, you came in. I didn't see anyone suspicious nor did I see Cowboy."

"Kendall! I watched him follow you across the street. Don't think for one second that we believe you didn't see him. You never miss anything."

"It's like I told Jack, I am not going to worry about this or try to figure it out. I don't think the guy is a threat. I think if we ignore him, he will go away or he will slip up."

Don was furious and said through clenched teeth, "Who is giving Jack this report?"

"I will. I will tell him you two think you saw Cowboy and I did not."

"Kendall, you are one of a kind."

59

Lindsay had a gut feeling something was not right as she headed for the courthouse and the hearing with Brad. She couldn't figure out exactly what it was. This hearing was another absurd accusation by Brad and just part of making her life hell. She wished the court would stop entertaining this level of crazy.

Lindsay had fired her attorney after the last hearing. She could have bought three houses with the amount of money she had paid him over the years. And she was no better off.

As she sat down on the bench outside the courtroom, Brad's attorney came over and asked, "Lindsay, you didn't hire another attorney? Are you seriously going to represent yourself?"

"Yes, Ted, if I may call you that. I noticed you called me by my first name. You don't like me having his last name any more than he does, huh? Lest you forget, I don't use his name, never did. At least legally. And yes, I'm representing myself."

"You know appearing in court without an attorney is like bringing a knife to a gunfight?"

"I will take my chances. Now, what can I do for you?"

"How do we make this go away?"

"Easy. Get your client under control. Oh, wait! You don't want to make this go away. He just paid you $5,000 for today's appearance. Business is so bad you need to take any and every case that comes your way, even if they are losing cases."

"Lindsay, seriously. How do we make this go away?"

"Ted, it's your client's Motion. I can't make it go away except through a Judge's ruling or your client's death. Do you have a golf game scheduled?"

"Can you ever be serious?"

"Not when I'm dealing with a bunch of clowns. We'll see what the Judge thinks of this latest funny business."

Upon entering the courtroom, Barbie appeared with baby brother. Lindsay ignored her, which of course just made Barbie furious.

After Ted gave his opening statement to the Court, Lindsay requested a verbal Motion to Dismiss based on no grounds for filing and no change of circumstances. The Judge denied and the court continued.

Lindsay hammered Brad on his financials so badly that it was embarrassing to the Judge and Ted. After being in Court for two hours, Ted finally asked for a 10-minute recess.

Coming back into the courtroom, Ted stated to the Judge that they would like to withdraw their Motion to the Court. The Judge asked for the reason to which Ted had no choice but to state that there were no grounds and no change of circumstances. The Judge asked Lindsay if she objected to which she replied "No" and refrained from saying, "I told you that two hours ago." She did, however, look over at Ted with a smirk.

The Judge stated that there were no grounds, nor could there ever be and if Mr. Daniels filed one more frivolous lawsuit, he would spend time in the local jail for harassment.

As Lindsay made her way to the door, she found herself side by side with Ted. "Ted?"

As he looked down at Lindsay with pure contempt but not saying anything, Lindsay said, "If you ever need my knife for one of your gunfights, I'll let you borrow it."

Ted was furious and stormed out with Brad and Barbie in tow.

As they reached the elevator, Lindsay looked at Brad and told him, "I know what you are up to. My attorney friend is also aware and should anything happen to me, you will be the first one arrested and questioned. And your sister-mother will be the next."

Brad went ghostly white and mumbled he would take the stairs and meet Ted outside.

"What the hell is that about, Lindsay?"

"Ask your client. I will tell you that should he not stop, I will file formal complaints against him and I'm on the verge of obtaining a witness. Tell him to stop."

Lindsay reached her car and felt complete satisfaction with the Judge's dismissal of this case and the warning about more frivolous suits. She felt relieved to finally say what she had long wanted to say to Brad. The bonus was saying it in front of his attorney. She felt quite happy about the whole morning.

Until she got in her car and saw the piece of paper blocking her speedometer. With a feeling of dread, she pulled it off and looked at it.

"Stay alert!" What the hell she moaned to herself. As much as Lindsay tried to maintain a "normal" life, others brought chaos to it. Just when she thought she had things figured out, she didn't.

60

Kendall had spent the last month staying low and doing as much research as she could from her computer that was on its own wireless network so nothing could be traced or hacked. She had kept the laptop with her everywhere she went to make sure it wasn't stolen. She wiped it clean after every use but she knew that those with highly technical skills could recover items, even though they had been deleted. She wasn't taking any chances. Everywhere Kendall went, so did her computer.

She hadn't seen much of Jack, avoiding him when possible and only talking to him on the phone when she had no choice. They were short, clipped calls. Kendall figured Jack was still angry with her. She was okay with that. She didn't want to see him right now.

She needed to take one more trip to Philadelphia. Her research had shown that Jack did live at the house on Langston Drive. The house next door to Jack in which they had all stayed during that one trip to

Philadelphia to try to pull Cowboy out was owned by Canfield, Inc. The same company that shows on her direct deposit paychecks. There wasn't much information on Canfield, Inc. It was a privately held company so their financials were not published.

Cowboy hadn't made any appearances in quite a while. It was discerning and she was hoping Jack hadn't gotten to him. Jack hadn't mentioned him either and that was not comforting. Maybe Jack believed her when she said she wasn't worried about him anymore.

As she made the drive to Philadelphia, she was rehashing everything in her mind. All the times she had seen Cowboy and all the contact, or lack thereof from him. Jack and all she knew about him. The companies that she had found including Langston Corp., Elle, Inc. and PJ Enterprises, Inc. Kendall wished her boyfriend were here and helping her. He was always her voice of reason and she had regretted not trusting him with what she was doing. She still missed him.

As she parked about a mile from Jack's neighborhood, avoiding the convenience store from last time, she pulled out her camera. Jack would have already left the office and should be home.

Kendall made her run past the convenience store and into the woods behind Jack's house. She never was a fan of the dark woods. As much as she liked going into buildings and homes under the cover of night, one would assume she liked the darkness. It was different in the woods. She had played in them when she was little and been scared by her older brother and his friends many times and had never gotten over the fear of the woods.

She slowed her run to a walk once she reached the wooded area. Coming up behind Jack's house, Kendall was relieved the lights were on inside. She assumed he was home, or someone was inside. Looking through the lens of her camera, she was disappointed to see all the blinds were closed.

Kendall turned and walked to the last house on Jack's street, making her way carefully through the trees. As she reached the side of the house at the end of the street, a dog began barking. She moved faster to the front, staying far enough away that anyone looking out wouldn't see her.

As she was watching the street view towards Jack's house, she noticed some of the cars in the driveways of the other homes were blacked-out Mercedes. There were two Camrys. Was there a meeting at Jack's or the house beside it?

Kendall crossed the street, going behind the houses opposite Jack's. She didn't like this because it left her a little exposed. The houses were back to back to the next street over. Most didn't have fences and the ones that did weren't adjoining others.

She made her way between the two houses that were almost directly across from Jack's. Kendall lay on the ground, watching Jack's and the one they stayed in last time she was here. It appeared nothing was going on in this neighborhood. Most of the houses had lights on but blinds closed.

Just as Kendall started to get up to move again, the

door to the house next to Jack's opened. She couldn't make out who came out but she knew the voices. Don, Joe, and others she worked with. She checked the flash on her camera just to be sure it was off and snapped a few pictures. She would hope they would show her more later.

As she lay there listening to their voices, there was one she didn't recognize, although it sounded vaguely familiar.

They all started walking down the street, some in one direction and some in the other. That didn't make sense. She got up and moved to the front corner of the house. Under the street lights, she recognized her co-workers in the organization.

Kendall watched as they each went into different houses along the street. What was going on? Did they all live here too? This made no sense. Granted, she didn't know much about any of them since it was protocol to keep things professional and they never got together except to work. Or maybe it was they never got together with her.

The last one to go into any house was Joe, their driver. She watched him walk into the last house on the same side of the street as Jack. It was the house she had to go by to get back to the woods. He had a dog. No wonder when it started barking no one came out to check. Joe wasn't there. He had been down the street. In a meeting. That didn't include her.

This was a revelation. No wonder they were all so close. They all worked together and were neighbors. She knew most of them had been with Jack for years but she had no idea they were this tight-knit.

This trip was definitely worth the ride. She stayed put in her position for a few more minutes. Then she made her way back towards the woods through the backyards from which she had come, then back across the street. This time she stayed in the woods beside the house, far enough back not to be heard by the dog. Joe's dog.

Just as she got almost to the backyard, she heard Joe's garage door open. She ran back in time to see him pull out of his driveway. Great. Now she didn't care if his dog barked.

Once Kendall cleared the backyard, she started making her way back to her car treading carefully through the woods. Suddenly, she heard something. She stopped dead in her tracks, holding her breath. She hated the woods.

"Don't move, don't make a sound."

She let her breath out slowly. She would know that voice anywhere.

She heard the click of his gun. Mass confusion welled up in her brain. Not Joe. Why would Joe pull a gun on her? Could Joe be the boss? No, that didn't make sense. Would Joe kill for the boss?

"Kendall, we are going to walk very slowly straight ahead and to your left. Don't try anything and I won't shoot you."

"Joe, please don't take me to Jack. He will kill me."

"I know. Move slowly."

Kendall's mind was reeling. What was going on? If

Joe knew she was here, did the others? She hated the unknown. Why was holding his gun on her? Surely, he wasn't going to kill her.

They had gone well beyond the convenience store, but still in the woods. Finally, Joe told her to stop walking and turn around.

Once she had turned around, Joe calmly said, "I'm putting my gun away. Don't try anything. We need to talk."

Kendall promised she wouldn't. She was glad to hear they were going to talk.

"Kendall, we know you are looking into Jack, the boss, and the companies. We know you are fixated with finding out who the boss is. What we don't know is why. Care to enlighten me?"

"Is this going back to Jack?"

"No. I promise you it is not."

"Why not? I know you have worked for Jack and the boss forever. I know how close you all are. Faithful and loyal is an understatement with this group."

"Kendall, answer my question."

"I would like to know who has controlled my life all of these years. I would like to know why I can't meet him, or her. I have always had a gut feeling there is more to this than Jack has ever told me. I was chosen. But why? There are others with my abilities. None of it makes sense. There is nothing logical to it. This gut feeling has been with me from the beginning. At first, I liked the mystery and intrigue. But it won't leave. It's like it's telling me I need to know more. It's important, although I don't know why."

"Your gut is right. But it's going to get you killed. Are you willing to die to get to the truth? Is there anything I can say or do to stop this? To put you at ease? If I tell you your gut is wrong, it's not going to be enough."

"No. You may not know much about me but you know I'm determined. You know I usually win. And if the truth is worth dying for, then all the more reason I need to know. It's personal now, Joe."

"That I do and that is why I am going to tell you what you want to know. If I tell you, will you stop hunting? Jack knows you have been at this for a while. The closer you get, the more dangerous it is for you. At some point, Jack will stop you."

"I don't understand how knowing who the boss is could get me killed."

"I will tell you what you want to know, about the companies, Jack and the boss. If I tell you and Jack ever finds out, he will kill both of us. If I don't tell you, I'm afraid you will get yourself killed. Do you understand what I'm saying? I like you. I always have. So does Jack. But he will stop at nothing to protect this organization. You could take it down, Kendall. You would be hurting a lot of people if you do anything with the information. You could destroy a lot of people's lives. I have to have your promise. If you don't stop with what I tell you and I find out you haven't, I will kill you myself."

"I don't understand how my knowing all of this is worth killing for. You all know. I'm no different than any of you."

"That's what I'm trying to tell you, Kendall. You are

different than the rest of us. We all were recruited. We all have specialized training. We all had a choice. You were chosen. You didn't have a choice. They would have gotten you one way or another. You can't say you won't do anything with the information, because you don't understand the extent of it."

"I understand that it will get me killed. I think that tells the importance. I promise. I don't want to hurt anyone. You do know that about me as well."

"Trust me, there is so much you don't know. This organization is international. We work with government agencies, criminal organizations, all of them. Most of what you have seen is mild compared to reality. You weren't taken deeper into the organization because we knew you were sidetracked with finding out information. There are others who don't want their secrets exposed and will kill to protect them. And you never know who is part of us. We are everywhere, in every occupation, in every region, in every city, state and country. This is so much bigger than you."

Did she have any other choice but to make promises on something she knew very little, if anything, about? Apparently, not. She'd never really been given choices.

61

Lindsay had lots of time over the next month to digest things. She processed it. She analyzed it. She thought about the consequences. She looked at it from every angle, then flipped it over and looked again. She hadn't been contacted by Cowboy or anyone else. It was like he never existed. Things were too quiet, except in her mind. She was surprised and a bit disappointed that she hadn't figured things out so much sooner. The only thing she wasn't completely sure of, was whose phone number was written on that piece of paper Tim had given her.

At 5:30 a.m., she dialed the number that Tim had given her, in case of an emergency. It was picked up on the first ring but nothing was said. She waited for one minute. Still nothing. She hung up. It didn't matter.

She grabbed her purse, her gun and locked the door behind her. She got into her spare car down the street and drove off.

At 6:15 am, Kendall was glad the sun hadn't risen yet. This time of year, it wouldn't until about 7:30. That's why she requested this meeting with Jack so early. Darkness would be her friend for once. Jack was a few minutes late and Kendall was already inside when he got to his office.

"How did you get in without setting off the alarm?"

"Is that how you greet everyone instead of good morning?"

"How did you get in without setting off the alarm?"

She waved her phone at him. "Technology is great. Good morning, Jack."

"Kendall, this better be important to get me here so early. I'm usually just getting up. I need more coffee."

"I already made a pot. I'm on my third cup." She handed him a cup. "It's how you like it."

"Ok, Kendall, what's going on? Why this early meeting? The sun isn't even up yet."

"You know I am very fond of you. You know I've

trusted you most of my life, as long as I've known you. I've even looked up to you."

"Kendall, this is very warm and fuzzy, which you are not. Get to the point."

"My, but you are grumpy in the morning. I would have taken you for a morning person."

"You know I don't like games."

"Ok, fine. I'll honor your request because it will be the last time I ever do."

Jack just looked at her with a blank face, but she could read his eyes. Outside he was cool as could be. It was his eyes that gave away the internal chaos. Kendall kind of liked seeing him squirm for once.

"I know what you've done. I know who you are. I know what you have been trying to protect all these years. I don't care. What I do care about is the one thing I've always cared about. The boss. Take me to him. Now." Jack didn't miss Kendall's fingernails digging into her palms.

"Kendall, I think the last few years have finally taken their toll on you. You aren't well. Sit down and let's talk about this."

"Jack! I'm not going to sit down on this one. I am sure I am right and there is nothing, nothing you can say to convince me otherwise. Now take me to him immediately or I'll slit your throat right here!" She had never meant anything more in her life. And Jack knew it.

"Kendall, you have done some crazy things and thought some crazy things in your time, but nothing this insane! Do you hear yourself? This is over the top, even for you!" And Kendall knew he spoke the truth and still she knew she was right. There would be no other reason for Jack to draw his gun on her, ever.

Kendall had stared Jack in the eyes the whole time he was speaking and she hadn't missed his hand slide to his gun. "Jack, if you kill me, the boss won't be happy. And others know the truth and they will do more damage to you than I will. Put that away before you get hurt."

Jack just stared at her, processing what she had said. "Who knows, Kendall? Tell me who you told your crazy, wild ideas to?"

"It doesn't matter. You are better off with me because as I said, I don't care about you. They do. Put the gun down Jack and let's go."

"Tell me what you know." Jack still had his gun pointed at her.

"I know that you and the boss have several companies, such as Langston Corporation who owns PJ Enterprises and Elle, Inc. I know who owns all the houses on the block in Philadelphia where we stayed when you sent me up there looking for Cowboy. Except for the one next door that is owned by the same company that writes my check. I know that the three companies own several cars, including identical Mercedes and Camrys and a helicopter in Philadelphia. I know that you and the boss created this company when I was still a small child. I know that there have been several "accidents" that caused deaths. Those deaths changed people's lives, Jack, including mine. I know that you contract work with Federal Agencies and the Mexican Cartel along with groups in other parts of

Central and South America along with a few European agencies. Good and bad. Again, I don't care about that. I will say there are a few questions I have not been able to figure out. Like who Cowboy is and if you had anything to do with my boyfriend's death last year. You found out he was going to propose, didn't you? You didn't like how close he was getting to me. I can't link you to his death, but if I do Jack, you will die a slow death."

"My you have been busy, Kendall."

"Yes, and as I said, I don't care about any of it. Are you taking me or do I have to let the others loose?" Kendall was bluffing. There were no others.

Before Jack could answer, a gun was fired right behind Kendall at the same time as she was grabbed and pulled down to the floor. A second gun went off. She felt the bullet breeze past her shoulder as she was being pulled down. Even though it happened in a split second, she was able to comprehend the feelings that those arms around her and the body pressing up against her caused.

She lay perfectly still, trying to breathe. Not because of the fall or the bullet, but because of the feelings going through her body.

She heard a voice that sounded vaguely familiar. "I have his gun. He'll live." Then she heard a voice that brought tears to her eyes. She couldn't move. She didn't want it to be a dream.

"Are you okay? Talk to me!" he practically screamed as he lifted her to a standing position.

It all happened so fast. She stood up with his help. She saw Jack on the floor, alive, but in horrendous pain. Then the tall figure standing over him. In a cowboy hat and boots. She slowly turned around to the one still holding her from behind. She just stared into the most beautiful face she had ever seen.

As soon as he realized she was okay, he broke out into that grin. "I've missed you, pretty lady."

This had to be a nightmare. Her brain wasn't processing that Sam was standing in front of her, with his arms holding her up, talking to her and sending shivers throughout her body. Was she dead too?

She recoiled as if she had been scorched with a hot branding iron. Silent tears slid down her face. For the second time in her life, she was speechless with silent tears. And both times involved Sam.

The past year after Sam's death had been the most

difficult of her life. She picked the phone up several times a week to call him. Then remembered. She had times when she couldn't breathe from missing him. She had times she thought she would die from a broken heart. She had times she was angry he was gone.

And now that he was standing in front of her, she was angrier than she had ever been in her life.

"How? Why, Sam?"

"I will explain everything to you but right now you have somewhere else to be. They are expecting us. Come on. We'll talk on the drive there."

She still couldn't move. He gently took hold of her again and lead her out the back.

As Sam and Cowboy loaded Jack into the SUV, Kendall was still in shock. She was having a hard time breathing, partly from Sam being this close and partly from everything that was happening. She had not planned for this. How could she?

After Cowboy put Jack in the backseat and his seatbelt on, he went around the front of the SUV. He threw the keys to Sam, "Guess you're driving." He got in the backseat on the opposite side of Jack, behind Kendall.

Kendall, with Sam's help, slid into the front passenger seat. Sam helped her get into her seatbelt, then as if in slow motion, put his hands on her cheeks and wiped some of the tears. "It's going to be okay now. You are safe." He gently closed the door and ran around the front of the SUV and slid into the driver's seat.

He started the SUV, looked at Cowboy over his shoulder, and asked: "You good?"

"Yup, let's roll."

Sam looked at Kendall and his face softened. Their eyes locked for a moment. Kendall had never seen so much love on anyone's face before. How could she be mad? If not for the feeling of being on the verge of vomiting, she would have expected to be awoken at any minute.

As Sam started driving, Kendall couldn't say anything. There were too many questions swirling in her head at the same time.

"Kendall, it's nice to meet you…formally. I'm Derek Stevens. I know you all have been calling me Cowboy. I'm not. I'm just Derek. Never wore a cowboy hat until this." He reached up and patted her shoulder from the backseat.

"Go ahead and start filling her in. We have a lot to tell her before we get there." Sam looked over at Kendall as he said it and gave her a wink along with a gentle smile. He was trying to soften the blows that he knew were coming.

Derek was all too eager. "Let me start with how I know Sam. We were Special Forces together. We became very close during our time together. Like brothers."

Jack grimaced. "I checked. Although I didn't have your name, you were never in pictures together."

"Shut it Jack or I'll let you bleed out before we get there. I don't do pictures. I already had a job when I got out and avoided them. There are no pictures of me. At least voluntarily. My job was with the boss. He made me the offer before I went in, fresh out of school. You see, Jack, the boss didn't completely trust you. He trusted you with everything and everyone, except Kendall."

Sam looked at her and grinned as he said, "I wouldn't trust many with her either."

Kendall looked at Sam with a tender smile, and thought "Oh, how I have missed that grin!"

Derek didn't miss the exchange between them but continued explaining anyway. "While I was in, Sam and I became best of friends, brothers, and I knew if I ever needed to bring someone in, he was my guy. I didn't plan for him to fall in love though." Derek let out a whistle. "That wasn't part of the plan."

"So, wait, you meeting me was no accident? This was prearranged? I should have known." Sam could see the anger spark in those beautiful green eyes.

Sam let out a long breath and in an almost pleading tone asked, "Please let Derek finish before you make any judgments. Can you do that? Please?"

She just looked at him and told Derek to continue.

Derek continued. "I was employed for the sole purpose of watching over you without getting close to cause Jack suspicion. I did that well. Until you started researching the boss and the rest. Until I could see Jack getting out of control with you. The first mistake didn't sit well with me. I couldn't get close enough to you with Tall One around. He was a loose cannon. We were happy you took care of that yourself. I... we, needed someone closer to you. That's when we hired Sam. It was twofold. He could get close to you and it would keep Jack at a distance by not providing you with more unstable covers."

Kendall was furious. "So, Sam, you were to get close to me? You certainly did that and played it well.

Congratulations. I hope there was a big bonus for you."

Sam looked at her with so much tenderness, it almost made her lose her anger. "You know I love you. There is no way to fake what we had. Have. None of us planned that. As a matter of fact, it put a strain on everything, including your safety. On one hand, it made things a lot tougher. On the other, it made them a lot easier. It wasn't part of the plan. I had no idea that I would fall in love with you the moment I set eyes on you. And it isn't just your beautiful face. I saw you in pictures first."

Then Derek spoke again, "We specifically had a meeting and considered taking Sam off this. I admit I was mad as hell when he told us after the first day he met you. None of us saw that coming. But then you don't really see true love coming. It hits you like a freight train when you least expect it." Derek said the last part so softly, she almost didn't hear it.

Sam looked at her with such sadness it instantly took away her anger. "I was going to be with you one way or another. I also quit taking money from them. It wasn't about the money. It was no longer a job."

Jack grimaced again. Kendall turned in her seat and looked at him. She felt sorry for him. Not because he was in pain from the gunshot, but because she had cared for him and he had at one time, been one of the very few people who cared for her during her late teens and early adulthood.

She looked back at Sam. "Still so many questions. But to clarify, Jack was carelessly playing fast and loose with my life, hoping but not hoping, something would happen to me?"

"Early on, no. Later, yes. He knew you were always curious about the boss but it was when you started looking into it seriously and taking trips to Philadelphia. He knew you were close. Some of the things were to scare you but inefficient. Like the two attackers on that one job that came out of a door that wasn't on the floor plans. One of the guys knew Jack had switched them. The door was added after the plans he showed you. The attackers were hired by Jack. He underestimated you."

"I will give you credit, Kendall. It took me a while to figure out it was you at the airport. I thought I had spotted you on my way out once. I looked at the camera captures. It was a female figure. Then it made sense."

"All of this was to stop me from finding out who the boss is?" Kendall was staring out the window. She was so deep in thought she didn't realize where they were going.

Anger rose in her at the same time she thought sadness would consume her. She was angry because of all that was taken away from her and she was sad for the same reason.

"I know this is a lot to take in. Are you okay so far?" Sam said it with so much tenderness and concern it almost overwhelmed her.

"I'm okay. I figured out most of what you are telling me already. Except for the parts concerning you. I figured Cowboy, sorry, Derek, was hired by someone watching out for me. I wasn't sure who or why. I didn't think it was protection from Jack, at least at first."

65

"Now that we are all up to speed, can you tell her that I didn't kill you so I can at least have a clear conscious on something before I die." Jack said this very slowly and between teeth gnashed in pain.

Sam looked at Jack through the rear-view mirror without expression. Then he glanced over his shoulder at Derek.

She turned in her seat to look at Jack. They were far from up to speed. She couldn't read his face through the apparent pain. "You aren't going to die. Yet. You may still if they don't confirm this." Out of the corner of her eye, she could see Sam's face. It was filled with pain.

Derek cleared his throat. "It was my idea. After the close call from Jack, we had to do something drastic to throw him off."

"What close call?" Kendall had so many questions and their answers just led to more questions.

Sam glanced over at her as he slowed for the traffic congestion ahead. "One of the times I ghosted you was because I was pretty banged up after a car accident. Someone cut the brake lines in my truck. I was unconscious for a few days. When I came to, I was badly bruised and not moving very easily. I was no good to you and you would have had too many questions that I didn't want to answer. I didn't want to lie to you."

"You didn't want to lie to me? Isn't this whole thing a lie? Isn't my whole life a lie?" She didn't recognize her own voice. For the first time in her life, she felt as though she was suffocating.

Sam wanted nothing more than to pull over, take her in his arms and hug her until neither could stand and he could consume all her hurt. "No. Please believe that."

Jack laughed in the backseat and Derek jabbed him next to the gunshot wound.

Derek continued. "We didn't think Jack knew Sam was working for us but thought he didn't like Sam around because he made you harder to get to. Jack wasn't sure if you had told Sam what you were doing. Really doing."

Sam started to talk then stopped. He couldn't look at her with that much pain on her face. He felt himself choking up.

"I started making appearances to you and messing with Jack to take the attention off Sam. I was also worried that Jack would kill both of you when you were together. No offense, but sometimes when Sam was with you, he was so focused on you and your safety, he forgot his own. I was able to stay closer to you and it was too dangerous with Sam and you together. I killed Sam. I

286

hired two of my buddies and the rest is what little you were told."

She looked at Sam. "Does Tim know? You could have just broken up with me?"

"No, Tim doesn't know. No, I couldn't just break up with you. It killed me when I disappeared on you, sometimes for very good reasons like the car accident, but as long as I was breathing, I wanted to be with you. If you thought I was dead, I couldn't come and go and put you in more danger. We assumed Jack also thought my death took your mind off finding out who the boss is."

"Did you make calls to me without saying anything?"

Before Sam could answer, Derek piped up again from the backseat. "No. That was Jack. We had a trace on your phone and they went back to a disposable phone. He was probably trying to get you to say something or see if you would say anything. The first time I was at your house, I put cameras up outside."

"Whose phone number was it that you gave to Tim at…. whose number did you give to Tim?" She was having a hard time breathing let alone talking. She thought of Tim and how he would take this.

Derek let out a groan. "That was the boss's phone number to a phone that he only uses for me and Sam. He kept that phone on him twenty-four hours a day and knew that if there was a number other than one of us, it was you. We knew about your car down the street. It has a tracer on it also. We had someone else follow you because we headed straight to Jack's office figuring that was where you were going. We came through the neighboring office through the storage room." Derek was doing most of the talking and answering.

Derek grinned at Sam in the rear-view mirror. "It was tough keeping him from you. I was glad that you traveled so he could keep an eye on Jack and I could follow you so in that regard it made my job easier."

Jack grimaced again and let out a little cry of pain when he tried to readjust himself in the seat. "How did you know where Kendall was going to be? Dallas, San Diego, Indiana?"

Derek laughed out loud. "Should we tell him?"

Sam glanced at Derek in the rear-view mirror and grinned. Not a special grin but a grin. "No, he'll find out in a minute since we're here."

"Kendall, would you like to have the honors of telling Jack how I knew where you were going to be when you traveled?" Derek gave her a minute to think about it.

"Is he here? He is going to kill me himself!"

"Yes, he's here and no, he's not. He's on my payroll, the boss's payroll."

"No, let him see for himself." She blinked a few times to clear her misty eyes and realized they were at Jack's house in Philadelphia. She started to get out when Sam asked her to stay seated for a minute while he helped Derek get Jack out.

66

Sam got back in the driver's seat and closed the door. He turned sideways to face her. "I'm sorry. I'm sorry for everything you've been through. If I could take it all back or fix it, I would. I'm not sorry that I met you or fell in love with you. I'm sorry that time was wasted that we could have been together. I'm sorry that you were lied....that I lied....I hope you can forgive me."

She looked at him for a long time. "There are things that could have been done so differently. There are things that I should have had a say in. Not just with Jack but with you. And my life."

"Yeah. You're right. It's going to take you a while to process all of this and I understand that. I want to help you do that. I will always be here for you." He used to be able to tell what she was thinking. But now too many things had happened. He hated not knowing what she was thinking. "From this second until the last breath I take, I will never leave you again."

Sam didn't realize he was holding his breath until she looked at him and gave him a small, but sad smile. He noticed too that her green eyes looked a little haunted. The spark he used to see in them was gone.

"Is the boss here?"

"Yes. Are you ready?" Sam didn't miss that she didn't respond to what he had just said. He knew she had more to take in before she could start to process all that had happened and all that was still to happen.

She closed her eyes and let out a deep breath. "Only one way to find out."

He came around and helped her out of the SUV. He held her hand as they walked to the door.

As they entered the house, she saw Joe sitting on the couch and Derek sitting in a chair. No one else was there. They both got up and walked over to her.

Joe didn't say anything. He looked her over to make sure she was still in one piece then hugged her and said in her ear, "I'm glad you are okay. I'm sorry I didn't tell you the whole truth."

She thanked Joe and looked at Sam as he took her hand.

Sam squeezed it. "Do you want me to go in with you?"

"No. I have to do this myself."

Derek nodded his head towards the hall and said, "End of hall on the right."

She walked down the hallway slowly. She had never had so many conflicting emotions going through her at one time. She reached the end of the hall, turned right and walked into the room.

She slowed her pace even more once through the door but continued walking almost to the center of the room. The boss stood beside a desk near the back of the room. With no hesitation, she said, "Hi Daddy."

He didn't move. He was as still as a statue. He had prayed this day would never come. There was too much to explain and it was all extremely complicated. It would also put her in danger if others found out their connection. He didn't think she would understand. They stared each other down for what seemed like forever.

"What's wrong, Daddy? You don't know whether to call me Lindsay or Kendall? We are the same person, remember?"

THE END

Did you enjoy *Parallel*?

Please consider leaving a review wherever you
purchased this book.

For more information on the Truth or Die Series and
future books, please follow Alex Clayborn at www.
authoralexclayborn.com.

ABOUT THE AUTHOR

ALEX CLAYBORN

Alex Clayborn has two grown daughters and has lived from northern Maine to southern Florida and many states in between. Alex's hobbies include traveling, downhill skiing, anything on top of the water and reading a good mystery novel. Alex has an accounting degree and worked in the forensic accounting field for many years, loving the chase of uncovering assets that people try to hide.

www.authoralexclayborn.com

 facebook.com/authoralexclayborn

Made in the USA
Monee, IL
26 November 2020

49679239R00176